D1048338

The Deadliest Blessing

A Provincetown Mystery

Jeannette de Beauvoir

best wishes,
Jeannette

HOMEPORT PRESS

Praise for
The Deadliest Blessing

"When Provincetown wedding coordinator and amateur detective Sydney Riley discovers a decomposed corpse in her elderly Portuguese neighbor's wall, the sins of the past reach out to the present and stir up long-dormant passions. Sydney's investigations lead her back to the Summer of Love hippie-era when drug- and alcohol-fueled tensions ran high and the families of fishermen and hard-living writers mixed with often-dire results. Sifting through tales from those long-ago days, Sydney must learn the identity of the killer before those who know the truth are silenced. At the same time, Sydney's boyfriend Ali, an ICE officer, is investigating a dangerous human trafficking ring. The action boils over in a shocking climax during the annual Blessing of the Fleet. de Beauvoir seamlessly blends fact and fiction, past and present, as "the tired, the lonely, even the misfits" of Land's End grapple with guilt in the third installment of this riveting mystery series."

—Debra Lawless is the author of the two-volume history of Provincetown--*Provincetown Since World War II: Carnival at Land's End*

"Wedding planner Sydney Riley is smart, funny, slightly quirky, and destined to find dead bodies in the strangest places. In *The Deadliest Blessing*s she faces witches, magic, and murder that keep her—and the reader—guessing. Toss in the unique Provincetown culture, a fundamentalist Muslim police commissioner, and a sympathetic ICE boyfriend, and you've got a page-turner to the end!"

—Janice Zarro Brodman, author, *Sex Rules!: Astonishing Sexual Practices and Gender Roles Around the World*

Other Books
by
Jeannette de Beauvoir

Mysteries:
In Dark Woods
The Provincetown Theme Week mysteries:
> Death of a Bear
> Murder at Fantasia Fair

The Martine LeDuc series:
> Deadly Jewels
> Asylum

The Trinity Pierce series:
> Murder Most Academic (as Alicia Stone)

Historical Fiction:
Our Lady of the Dunes
The Crown & The Kingdom

The Deadliest Blessing: A Provincetown Mystery
Copyright © 2018 by Jeannette de Beauvoir

Published by HomePort Press
PO Box 1508
Provincetown, MA 02657
www.HomePortPress.com

ISBN   978-0-992451-4-9
eISBN 978-0-99992451-5-6

Cover Design by Miladinka Milic

The poem "Missing" is copyright © 2002 by Oona Patrick and is re-printed by permission of the author. It was first published in *Paragraph*, vol. 8, n. 1, fall 2002, by Oat City Press.

The Deadliest Blessing is a work of fiction. Names, characters, places, situations, and incidents are the products of the author's imagination and used fictitiously. Any resemblance to actual events, locales, or persons, living or dead, is purely coincidental.

All rights reserved. No part of this eBook/Book may be reproduced or transmitted in any form or by any means, electronic or mechanical, including photocopying, recording, or by any information storage and retrieval system, without permission in writing from the publisher.

This book is licensed to the original purchaser only. Duplication or distribution via any means is illegal and a violation of International Copyright Law, subject to criminal prosecution and upon conviction fines and/or imprisonment. This eBook/Book cannot be legally loaned or given to others. No part of this eBook/Book can be shared or reproduced without the express permission of the publisher.

Missing

Missing: one drowned man's wooden leg, a lifering, a tow rope, a storm anchor, Rebecca Burch's grave stone, whales and boat brushes, vinyl, oilskins, foul weather gear, lobster pots, a trap, a net, the secret formula for artificial brownstone, the hands of a murdered woman, the church's steeple, the church's stained glass windows, the church's congregation, a buried car, a load of booze sunk in a pond, a load of pot sunk in a boat, trees from traffic islands, my dog Max, one million seed clams, the tenant, the young poet, the lovers down the street, Rocky, Bessie, Annie, Jason, Tiss, Begunna, Uncle Powerful, and the 10,000 Menangases, the words sabe não sabe, a fisherman in a fogbound dory, the Somerset's timbers, the safe off the Portland, an old man's sight, Mrs. Dorothy Bradford, a shipload of lumber, a shipload of coffee, a shipload of linen, the town hall on the hill, the first plaque to the Pilgrims, the Alabama Claim, the sailor's valentine, the schooners, brigs, and barques, the John Adams, the Panama, and the Mermaid, Catholicism and the family Bible, an old man's memory, the town crier, the bowling alley, Whaler's Wharf, and the shoals and shoals of silver fish, so thick we thought we might one day walk the bay.

- Oona Patrick

1

The sunset was living up to expectations.

I'd parked my Civic—known affectionately as the Little Green Car—in the row of vehicles facing Herring Cove Beach, one of the few places on the East Coast where the sun appears to set into the water. As usual, the light was spectacular. It's the light that made Provincetown what it is, the oldest continuously operating art colony in the United States: the light here, apparently, is like nowhere else.

Or so my friend Mirela tells me. She's a painter, and is constantly talking about the light, though when it really comes down to it, she can't explain exactly what it is they all see, the artists who live and work here. I know; I've asked.

It was late spring, and I didn't yet have too many weddings crowding my daily calendar, so I was taking advantage of the calm before the storm of the summer tourist season really hitting when my spare time, like everybody's else's, would disappear altogether. I'm the wedding coordinator for the Race Point Inn, and while we do tasteful winter weddings inside the building, the bulk of my work is in the summertime, as Provincetown is pretty much Destination Wedding Central, mostly for same-sex couples but really for anyone who wants this kind of light. The sun was carving a path of gold right up to the beach, glittering and gilded, and I knew I was smiling, settling back into my seat with a sigh.

My phone rang.

Cell coverage is spotty out here in the Cape Cod National Seashore, and my experience is that it's when you really need to reach someone that it's not going to happen; on the other hand, when it's something you *don't* want to deal with, the signal comes through loud and clear. Murphy's Law, or something along those lines. I sighed and swiped, my eyes still on the sunset. "Sydney Riley."

"Sydney, hey, hi, it's Zack."

My landlord. This couldn't be good. I mentally checked the date. Um, I'd paid my rent this month, right? "Hi, Zack."

"Hey, hi. Listen, Sydney, I've got Mrs. Mattos here and she's looking for you."

Of course she was. I live above a night-club, which makes for reasonable rent with free Lady Gaga thrown in at one o'clock in the morning; Mrs. Mattos is the eighty-something widow who owns the very large house directly across the street. Property developers are probably checking on her health daily as they wait for her demise; I can't imagine how many million-dollar condos they could create in that space.

I take her grocery shopping to the Stop & Shop once a week and I've noticed, lately, that she's finding more and more excuses to come over and buzz my doorbell. She's lonely and probably a little scared and most of the time I try to help, but the silly season was already upon us and there was a lot less of my time available. Generally I try to wean her off daily visits by May, but we were already into the beginning of June now, and she was crossing the street rather than calling, a sure sign of distress.

Mrs. Mattos is frequently distressed.

Still, it must have been something out of the ordinary for her to have buzzed Zack, who owns the nightclub as well as the building and was probably peeled away from his never-ending paperwork to talk to her. Mrs. Mattos is usually a little nonplussed around Zack, who regularly paints his fingernails chartreuse or purple, and owns an extensive assortment of wigs. "She's there with you now?"

A murmur of conversation, then Mrs. Mattos' quavering voice on the line. "I just need you to come over, Sydney," she said.

The sun was dipping into the water now; the show would soon be finished. Above it, scarlet and pink streaked across the sky. Some day, I told myself, I was going to be old and quavering, too. "Okay, you go back home," I said. "I'll be there in twenty minutes."

Her name is Emilia Mattos, she stands about five-feet nothing and might weigh a hundred pounds. But every bit of her, like most of the Portuguese women in town, is muscle and sinew. I know her first name, but I've never used it; there's a certain distance, a certain decorum the elderly Provincetown widows observe, and I respect that. Out on Fisherman's Wharf there's a collection of large-scale photographs of elderly Portuguese wives and mothers, an art installation called They Also Face The Sea; Mrs. Mattos isn't one of them, but she could well be.

Back when Provincetown was one of the major whaling ports, ships stopped off in the Azores to take on additional crew, and a lot of those people settled back in town and sent for their families; by the end of the 1800s they were as numerous as the original English settlers. Nowadays there are fewer and fewer Portuguese enclaves, as gentrification switches into high gear and Provincetown's fishing fleet dwindles; but the names are still here: Santos, Avellar, Cabral, Gouveia, Silva, Amaral, Rego, Nunes.

Up until about ten years ago, a prominent advertisement in the booklet for the Portuguese Festival was for the small Azores Express airline, when there was still a generation in town that was from Portugal itself; you don't see that anymore.

She was standing in her doorway when I found a parking place for the Little Green Car and got to our street. I've read in books about people twisting their hands; I'd never actually seen it until then. "Mrs. Mattos! Are you all right? What's wrong?"

"Probably nothing," she said, on that same quavering note. "Oh, I'm probably disturbing you for nothing, Sydney."

"Not at all," I said firmly, taking hold of her elbow and turning her around. "Let's go in, and you can tell me all about it."

She was docile, letting me steer her back in the house and into the big kitchen where most of her life seems to take place. She has a home health aide who comes in to help her with bathing and laundry, but she doesn't let anyone touch her stove: not to cook, not to clean. And when I say clean, I mean clean within an inch of its life: everything in Mrs. Mattos' kitchen gleams. Not for the first time, I lamented that she couldn't make it up my stairs: if she expended about an eighth of her usual zeal, my apartment would be cleaner than it had ever been.

She sat down, still fussing with her hands. "I'm having construction work done," she said, and stood up again. "I should show you."

"What kind of work?"

"Insulation." Her voice was repressive, as if she were delivering censure of something. We'd just come off an amazingly, spectacularly cold winter, with single-digit temperatures and a nor'easter that brought the highest tides ever recorded, so I suspected she wasn't the only one thinking about making changes. "In the walls. Them people at the Cape Cod Energy said I should."

"Okay." I still wasn't getting what was wrong here. "Do you want to show me?"

She turned and led me into the front parlor (in Mrs. Mattos' house, you don't call it a living room); I had to duck to get through the heavy framed doorway, and the ceiling here was about an inch or so over my head. She, of course, had no such problems. A loveseat had been pulled away from one of the exterior walls and a significant hole made. She didn't have drywall, but rather plaster and lathing, as older houses tended to. "There wasn't nothing wrong with it. The insulation before was just fine," she said, resentful. "Seaweed."

"Seaweed?"

She nodded vigorously. "Dried out. It's what they used." No need for anything else, her tone suggested.

"Okay," I said again. "What is—"

"Go look," she said, flapping her hands at me. "Just look."

I looked. I pulled my smartphone out of my pocket and used the built-in flashlight. Wedged between strips of lathing was a box. "Is this it?"

Mrs. Mattos blessed herself. "Holy Mother of God," she said, which I took for assent.

"Can I take it out?" I asked, eyeing the box. It looked as innocuous as last year's Christmas present. Well, maybe not last year's. Maybe from sometime around 1950.

Another quick sign of the cross. "Just don't make me look. I can't look again."

I put my smartphone in my pocket and reached gingerly into the opening. Didn't Poe write a story about a cat getting walled up somewhere? "Who's doing your work for you, Mrs. Mattos?" It didn't look as though they'd gotten very far in opening up the wall.

She was back to twisting her hands again. "The company wanted so much," she began, and I nodded. Rather than getting a contractor, pulling a permit, having a bunch of workmen in her house and paying reasonable rates, she'd found someone to do it on the side. Someone's unemployed cousin or nephew, probably. That sort of thing happens a lot in P'town, especially among the thrifty Portuguese. It explained the size of the hole, anyway: this was someone without a whole range of tools.

I pulled the box out—it was about the size of a shoebox, only square—and set it down carefully on the coffee table. Mrs. Mattos was looking at it as though something were about to pop out and bite her, like the creatures in *Alien*; she actually took a physical step back.

This wasn't just Mrs. Mattos being Mrs. Mattos; this thing was really spooking her.

I sat down beside the table and gingerly— you can't say that I don't pick up on a mood— lifted the top off the box. Sudden thoughts of Pandora blew by like an errant wind and I shook them off and looked inside.

Shoes; small shoes. Children's shoes. Three of them, and none matching the others. It was wildly anticlimactic. "Shoes?" I said, doubt—and no doubt disappointment—in my voice.

"It's not the shoes," she said. "It's that we shouldn't never have moved them."

I looked at them again. Old leather, dry and curling and peeling. But *shoes?* She was clearly seeing something I wasn't. Had these children died some horrible death? Were these memories of lives that hadn't been lived to their fullest? Something haunting, a song or an echo of laughter, moved through my mind as though on a whisper of summer air. I didn't recognize the tune. "Mrs. Mattos?"

"It's to keep them witches out," she said, grimly.

"Witches?"

She nodded. "An' now there's nothing to keep 'em from coming in. And nothing we can do about it, neither."

2

I was meeting Mirela at Mac's at four the next day for happy hour—oysters were only a dollar each, who can resist that?—which was a good thing, as Mirela is my sounding board for a lot of life situations. We sat at the bar and ordered beer and oysters. I could *live* on beer and oysters.

"So I want to ask you if you've ever heard of something," I began.

She pushed an errant bit of blonde hair off her forehead. Mirela is beautiful—as in, cover girl model beautiful—and is totally aware of it. It would be irritating if I didn't like her so much. "I have heard of every-thing," she said. "What do you think, I'm in-nocent?"

"Not something like *that*," I snapped. "This has nothing to do with sex."

"Everything has something to do with sex," she said.

"Not this," I said darkly. "This has to do with witches."

"Ah, my point exactly." She waited until Kate, the bartender, delivered the platter of oysters and went away. "Witches were perse-cuted because men couldn't handle the sexual natures of women," she said. "It's well known. At home, here, everywhere, women have always been a threat to men. That's why they were called witches."

"You have witches in Bulgaria?" Mirela came to Provincetown eight years ago and within three years of her one-summer-only plan had become a recognized painter, with a gallery on Commercial Street representing her and doing a brisk business because of it.

She shrugged. "Of course we have witches," she said. "Everyone has witches. Why do you want to talk about witches?"

"My neighbor is afraid of them," I said. "You know, Mrs. Mattos? Across the street from me? Somebody ripped a hole in her wall and found this box with shoes in it. Little baby shoes. And now she thinks she's not safe anymore."

She was staring at me. "Someone ripped a hole in her wall? Who would do such a thing?"

"She's having work done. She *meant* for them to rip the wall. And that's not the point," I said impatiently. "The point is that this box was in there and she's totally freaked out about it."

"Anyone would be," she said, dressing an oyster and dispatching it. "It's not easy to be safe."

"All right." I put down my glass with rather more assertion than I'd meant to. "Tell me everything you know about this. Tell me what you're talking about."

She sighed. "When people used to build houses, they put things in the walls before they plastered over them," she said, patiently, as though teaching something obvious to a recalcitrant child. "Or they lifted the floor and put things under the boards. To create an area of safety. A zone, you call it. Don't you ever read anything?"

"Obviously not the right things," I said. "When? Who did it?"

"Probably whoever built the house," she said. I waited while she put horseradish and hot sauce onto another oyster. "Everyone

12

was afraid," she said, finally. "People didn't understand about the world before science, about why you get sick, about what can kill you. No one understood the plague, or cancer, or anything like that. It was the evil spirits, they thought, and they wanted to keep themselves safe from evil. Like wearing a lucky charm, but instead, it was to keep your house safe, and the people inside it."

"And putting stuff in the walls did that? Created that safe zone?" Call me dense, but I still wasn't seeing the connection.

"It was a decoy, is that the right word? A way to send them somewhere else. To be protected from them." She signaled Kate for more beer, then turned back to me. "Oh! I know what it is like! It's like the people who make hats out of aluminum foil. To keep the aliens away."

"Talk about evolution," I murmured.

"Aliens are the evil spirits of our time," pronounced Mirela with satisfaction. "The same atavistic fears prey on people."

I didn't ask her where she got that word. Mirela has a far better vocabulary than most native English speakers. "So if you move the items out of the wall..."

"... you have invited the spirits to come back in!"

13

I shook my head. "Mrs. Mattos is Catholic. She sits in the front pew at St. Peter's every single Sunday," I said. "I can't see her believing in evil spirits and witches."

"Why not? They are in the Bible."

"You have an answer for everything, don't you?" I asked sourly. "The thing is, what to do about it now."

"Oh, no, sunshine," said Mirela, shaking her head. She thinks "sunshine" is a term of endearment. "The thing is, what else is in there?"

***

I got home early, with sunset only an enticing promise out to the west. I wasn't going to sunset tonight: it was time for an early night. I had a wedding at noon tomorrow, I hadn't slept well, and I also hadn't spoken to my boyfriend in a couple of days.

Well, I could do something about that last bit, anyway. I picked up my smartphone. "Hey, how's the big bad border patrol?"

"I don't do border patrol," Ali said. He hates it when I call it that. Granted, he works for Immigration and Customs Enforcement, an organization that will never get my vote as Nice Guys of the Year (and which *does* do border patrol, through being a part of Homeland Security), but he's in Human Trafficking. Or at least he is for now; that department burns them out fast.

He sounded tired, though, and I was instantly penitent. "Are you okay?"

"As okay as I ever am," he said. Yep: Ali was going to be looking for a new career path soon, for sure.

"Work?" I opened the refrigerator and peered in. Same stuff that had been there this morning. I don't know why I expect it to magically fill up with delicacies when I have my back turned.

"Work, yeah. And Karen."

"Karen?" That was unexpected. Ali's sister Karen is the Boston police commissioner. She was far more likely to worry about Ali than he was about her. I took out an apple and examined it. "Why?"

"Because she's gone off the deep end, that's why," he said, his voice sharp. The apple was past its prime. I put it back. Maybe it would look better tomorrow. "What deep end is that?"

Silence, which is fairly unusual with Ali. Then, "You know she was just in Beirut, right?"

His voice had taken on a different timbre, just a little off, like a sudden crack in a familiar bell. "On vacation," I said, nodding. Ali and Karen's parents came to the United States from Lebanon when the children were toddlers. They didn't go back frequently, but Karen often spent her vacations there, staying with relatives and practicing her Arabic.

"Yeah, well, this time was different."

I shut the refrigerator. "Different, how?" I opened the cupboard I use as a pantry. Maybe there were some Wheat Thins I'd forgotten. Nope. I was pretty sure that there was absolutely nothing in my house that I wanted to eat.

"When she came home," he said, and I could feel the panic running through his words, fast and electric, "she was wearing a headscarf."

Whoa. I slammed the cupboard door shut and turned and leaned against it. Ali and Karen are both Muslim, but in the same way I'm Catholic: it's how we all grew up, but then we grew out of it. The practice, anyway; I still have rosary beads somewhere and have been known to ask God for help in tight situations, but I haven't been to Mass in years. To the best of my knowledge, Ali doesn't even own a prayer rug. "You're kidding," I said, possibly one of the stupidest remarks I've ever made.

16

"She says she's been living a lie all this time," said Ali. "She says that she's been betraying her people and her religion." A pause, and then, in almost childlike wonder, "I always thought her people meant the police department."

I did, too: Karen loves the police. She'd worked her way steadily and quickly up through the ranks and was Boston's youngest-ever commissioner. She had occasional boyfriends, but that was all: she was married to the job. "What the hell happened in Beirut?"

"I don't know," he said, frustrated. "She won't say. She won't talk to me about it. She made it sound like I was somehow—unclean."

I didn't know what to say to that, so I seized on the most practical of details. "How can she wear a hijab with her uniform?"

"It's not *hijab*," Ali said forcefully enough for me to pull the phone away from my ear for a moment. "Calling it that is exactly what's wrong. It's—"

He broke off and I could hear him talking to someone else. When he came back, his voice was back to normal, too. "Sorry, Sydney. Have to go. I'll call when I can."

"Okay," I said, feeling a little dazed. "I love you." But he had already disconnected.

I found some cereal and sat down on the couch with it. (Well, okay, it's a loveseat; my apartment's not big enough for a couch.) Ibsen jumped up and did some exploratory circles and settled in next to me, purring loudly. And I sat and crunched my raisin bran and thought about things.

Witches and evil spirits and headscarf-wearing women. For someone who considered herself religion-free, I was getting into an awful lot of theology here.

3

Mrs. Mattos was back the next morning.

"I know you are tired of me," she began when I answered my door at 6:30, wearing my t-shirt and pajama bottoms, my hair its usual morning rat's nest. But, damn, six-*thirty*?

"What is it, Mrs. Mattos?"

She pointed across the narrow street to her house. "There's more in there," she said darkly.

I stared at her, feeling stupid. "More of what?"

"Things," she said, managing to make the word sinister and menacing.

I remembered, then, the box with the baby shoes in it. Meant to throw witches off the scent. "Did you find more shoes?" And who the hell was doing her construction work, anyway, that he couldn't be bothered to take this stuff out of there quietly without scaring an old lady half to death?

"You have to come," she said and then, as though to keep me from saying no, a torrent of words came out in a rush. "Please. I didn't hardly sleep last night, not a single wink, because of thinking of that hole and what's behind it, and it's not like I believe in all them spirits and such carrying on, because I don't, but it does feel different, my house does, now, an' I've slept there every night of my life after my wedding night, and it was there all the time and I never knew, and I wish I still never knew about it!"

"All right," I said, holding up a hand. "Give me five minutes, I'll be over." It was six-thirty in the morning and she had every hair in place and her uniform of skirt and blouse with a flowered apron on over it. She'd probably already waxed her kitchen floor and done a load of laundry and polished the silver. Next to her, I felt like a slug.

"I'll wait," she said.

"I promise I'll be right over. I need to get dressed."

She nodded. "I'll wait."

No one was moving Emilia Mattos if she didn't want to go. I surrendered to the inevitable and stood aside. "Come on in."

I went into the bedroom to find some clothes (preferably ones that hadn't been flung on the floor last night) and when I came out she was dusting. I swear it: she was *dusting*. "Mrs. Mattos?"

She gave the top of my desk a final glare and put the cloth in the cupboard under the sink. I held the door open for her again, and out we went.

It takes a while to cross the street when you're eighty-something, so we shuffled slowly along and I waited while she laboriously located keys in her apron pocket, decided on the correct one, and unlocked the door. This was Provincetown; I don't think I even *own* a key to my apartment, and she'd locked her door to go across the street. Okay. Different generation; different rules.

Through the kitchen and into the living room. Her guy had been at work; there still wasn't any insulation in the wall, but the hole was a lot bigger. I strenuously hoped that he wasn't charging her much for this. "Go on," she said, nodding.

With a strong sense of déjà vu, I headed over to the exterior wall, clicking on the

smartphone flashlight application. There was
the box with the shoes—and no one had yet
answered the obvious question of why
shoes?—and then, way beyond it, more stuff.
I had to wedge myself into the wall for my
beam to reach it, and talk about dust, this
place even beat out my apartment, and then
when I realized what I was looking at, I
screamed. Well, it was more of a squeal, actually, but I could be forgiven.

Wasn't I the one who'd remembered that
Poe story? Was it premonition? What was in
the wall was something dark and leathery like
the shoes, not enclosed in a box, and with a
head and a tail.

A cat. A mummified cat. I'd never be able
to look at Ibsen in quite the same way again.

I pulled my head and shoulders out of the
wall, fast. Mrs. Mattos was nodding. "Now
you see," she said, grimly.

"It's a cat," I said unnecessarily.

"It's a cat." We seemed to be in agreement on that point.

"What happened? Who could do that?"
As Ibsen's place in my life indicates, I'm very
fond of cats. I'm a cat person in a town filled
with dog people. It's almost a matter of
honor, now.

And then, as another thought occurred to
me, "You just saw this now?" Surely she

hadn't sat up all night with this in her wall, waiting until dawn so she could come and wake me?

Mrs. Mattos lowered herself onto one of her uncomfortable-looking chairs, an affair in wood and chintz with a whiter-than-white antimacassar on the back. "I seen it this morning," she said grimly. "When I went to clean up the mess that young Joe left me with in here last night." I looked back at the wall and saw it then, the little plastic caddy with cleaning products sitting on the floor beside the enlarged hole. Of course she knew how dirty it was in there; it must have been driving her mad. Joe—whomever he was—probably only came by after his day job was finished, hence the evening visit.

She'd probably seen the cat at something ungodly like four o'clock. In retrospect, she'd shown restraint in waiting until six-thirty to wake me. But the real problem was, I still couldn't see what kind of help I could offer. A blessing? Not my department. "Maybe," I ventured, "the priest over at Saint Peter's…"

"I'm not about to be bothering Father Mick with this!" It was as though I'd suggested taking her problem to the president.

"Okay." I hesitated. "What is it that you want me to do, Mrs. Mattos?"

She made the shooing gesture with her hands again. "Get rid of it! I can't be having dead animals in my walls!" No more talk now, I noticed, about losing any psychic protection; she was off the anti-witch campaign in a big way.

The thing was, I didn't feel warm and fuzzy about picking up that cat, myself, when it came down to it. I ran wildly through a list of people I knew who might be willing to do it, and I concluded that Mike and Glenn—the Race Point Inn's manager and owner, respectively—would think me crazier than Mrs. Mattos, crazier than they already thought me, if I asked. Ali would do it, but he was in Boston. The Zack option didn't even enter my mind. Damn.

What would we do with it? The last time I'd been near a dead cat it was Ibsen's predecessor in my life, Lily, and she'd just been euthanized at the vet's. She got placed in a box—with a baby blanket, a nice touch—and I'd taken her out into the National Seashore and buried her there. Illegal, of course. I wasn't risking getting caught doing that for this cat, whoever and whatever it had been in life.

That thought prompted a lot of questions. Had it been *alive* when it was walled up? How cruel was that? And if not, how had the house's residents dealt with the smell of its decomposing body?

Inquiring minds, in this case, really didn't want to know. I knew I was just putting off the inevitable. I looked at Mrs. Mattos and sighed. "I'll need some gloves," I said. She probably had a ten-pack of rubber cleaning gloves stashed away somewhere.

She did. I pulled on the big yellow rubber things and felt ready to do almost anything, except maybe retrieve a dead cat from a small confined space. *Breathe, Riley,* I told myself: my internal mantra for difficult times and anxious thoughts. *Just breathe.* I got the smartphone out and clicked on the flashlight. I wedged myself for a second time into the space between the lath and plaster and the wooden exterior wall. I took several deep breaths, and I cast the beam back toward the mummified body.

And stopped.

Deep breaths weren't going to help much, now. We had a bigger problem than a dead cat. We had a much bigger problem than a dead cat.

It wasn't the bright white that you'd expect, kind of brown and yellow and lumpy, but I was pretty sure that what the flashlight beam was picking up farther along the empty space was someone else who'd been keeping that cat company.

Only this one was human.

4

I called Julie right away.

Julie Agassi is the head of the detective unit in our small town. That doesn't mean that she doesn't do a lot of things that detectives in big cities don't get to do, like spending a shift on patrol; but she's the go-to person in felony cases. Which this might or might not be, but I wasn't taking any chances. At the very least it had to be illegal disposal of a corpse; it wasn't as if they'd run out of places up at the cemetery.

I'd had occasion to call on Julie in her professional capacity before. My first boss at the Race Point Inn, Barry, had been murdered—it still feels odd to say that—during one way-too-memorable Bear Week. And there'd been two deaths (with the potential for another, namely, myself) at a Fantasia Fair I'd never forget. So Julie and I aren't just friends; we have a professional history as well.

Mrs. Mattos and I stayed well clear of the wall while we were waiting. We sat in our separate chairs, and I tried to engage her in conversation a couple of times, but she wasn't having any of it. Things had gone from Very Bad with a dead cat in her wall to Infinitely Worse with a dead human, and she had taken about as much as she could take.

Julie wasn't happy about the early hour, either. "You've found another body," she repeated when I called her. "Seriously. You've found another body. Sydney, I hate to say it, but this is becoming a habit with you."

"It's not so much a body, as it *used* to be a body," I said, turning so that I didn't have to see Mrs. Mattos, who looked to be more affronted that there were going to be Police In Her House than she was at the bodies turning up in her wall. That was my impression, anyway.

"If it's over a hundred years old, it's considered archaeological," said Julie.

"And you want me to ask it how long it's been there?"

"Now you're doing it deliberately," she said. "All right, I'll be there. We'll probably have to send it out for dating, anyway."

"Anyone wants to date this guy, they have my blessing." When I'm nervous I get flippant. I've noticed that, inexplicably, very few people seem to appreciate said flippancy.

Julie certainly didn't. "Don't touch anything," she said. "I'll be there as soon as I can."

Which left me and Mrs. Mattos sitting in silence in the living room.

I tried to occupy my thoughts usefully. There was a wedding at noon, and I was going to have to be at the Race Point Inn by 10:30 to get things organized; fortunately it was a simple affair in the inn's terrace where we had a bower and chairs for the ceremony. The officiant and the photographer both were old hands at this, and there wasn't any family or friends invited; unless one of the two brides went off the rails, it would be simple. Ceremony, champagne toast—the champagne was already on ice and probably irritating the hell out of Adrienne, the inn's diva chef, who thought I should never ever *ever* set foot in her kitchen.

Having contemplated that, I started thinking about the Poe thing. It wasn't "The

Tell-Tale Heart," was it? But there was something similar, somewhere else… and then I had it. A man murders his wife and puts her in the wall, but the live cat is somehow accidentally in there with the body, and when the police come to investigate, the cat starts yowling and gives the hiding place away. That was it. He'd tortured the cat, or something. There was a lot more to it, but that was what I remembered.

I glanced at Mrs. Mattos. Best not to share the parallels with her. She'd probably never heard of Poe, anyway.

On the other hand, there was every possibility in the world that she did know exactly who the person—if not the cat—had been when they were alive. I didn't have all the details, but this house had been in the Mattos family for something approximating forever. Obviously no one had thought to mention, "oh, and by the way, don't open up the west wall, your Uncle Tommy is in there" on their deathbed, but every family has a secret or two, and family lore usually carries its black sheep's secret exploits from generation to generation.

Always assuming we'd just met the black sheep, of course.

It was probably less than an hour but felt like twenty when Julie arrived. She had a patrol officer with her and was in her uniform, looking very official and very unhappy. "I'm not even on this shift," she said by way of greeting.

"Neither am I," I said. I was getting tired of being blamed for finding bodies. It's not like I actually go *looking* for them.

Her eyes rested briefly on me. "Okay. Where is it?"

I couldn't bring myself to say, "in the wall." That sounded just a little too creepy. Instead, I gestured. "Maybe Mrs. Mattos can wait in the kitchen?"

"I'm staying here," Mrs. Mattos said firmly. This was becoming a spectacle, and she needed to be at the center of it. I could just imagine the reaction of her friends at church.

Julie's eyes rested on her briefly, then she turned back. "Show me."

She had a much better flashlight than the one on my smartphone, and she kept her head inside the wall for a long time. She didn't touch anything; I've noticed that about Julie, that she never touches anything at a crime scene. And why I've managed to get so much experience with crime scenes is beyond my understanding.

Finally she pulled her head out. "Can't tell," she said to me, then addressed the patrol officer. "We're going to need the medical examiner and probably a forensic anthropologist before we know for sure. Get that started."

He was scribbling madly in his notebook and left right away, depressing the microphone he carried on his shoulder and already talking into it as he exited the house. No one had gathered outside, yet, but it was still early: give it a little time. I pulled the lace curtains firmly closed and perched on the edge of my chair again.

Julie sat down beside Mrs. Mattos; she'd had the same thought I did. "Did you have any idea there were human remains there, Emilia? Do you know who that might be?"

I was more shocked by her use of Mrs. Mattos' first name than I was by her asking such a direct question. Julie was lucky she was a detective. Mrs. Mattos would have taken anyone else's head off for doing that.

She was already shaking her head. "No."

"There are some other things in there," I said helpfully. "Things meant to ward off evil spirits and keep the witches away." I couldn't wait to hear how Julie was going to respond to *that*.

She didn't. "The obvious question," she said, "is how this person ended up behind the wall."

"I'd have thought the obvious question was who put them there," I said.

Julie glared at me. Mrs. Mattos glared at me. I wasn't making myself very popular, and to hell with this: I had a wedding business to run. I stood up and made a show of dusting off my knees. "I'll be off, then," I said.

"No," said Mrs. Mattos, with a look of don't-leave-me-with-her. I wasn't fooled. Over the past couple of days I'd been letting her get away with a lot of Old Lady stuff when it was clear that her brain was far more spry than she'd wanted me to believe.

"Okay," said Julie, who was probably wishing that she'd been on vacation this week, far away from Provincetown and everyone's favorite wedding planner and finder of dead bodies.

"And who," demanded Mrs. Mattos, "is going to pay for all of this?"

I left them to it and fled.

***

To my complete surprise, the wedding went well. I think I'd been expecting something dire, as though the morning's events were meant to color the rest of the day. The string quartet from the Cape Cod Symphony was on time. The photographer was finding brilliant angles to take pictures, and the couple was thrilled before they even got there. The officiant gave them a lovely ceremony, the two brides sipped champagne appreciatively, and one of them got a little weepy. Then they left to meet friends at MacMillan Pier and the schooner I'd reserved for their reception, and I got to relax a bit.

There was a new receptionist at the Race Point Inn, a particularly pretty boy in a town that, in season, is filled with pretty boys. Provincetown is a lot of things—an art colony, a still-operating Portuguese fishing village, a center for marine biology—but in the summer, more than anything, it's a gay resort. His name was Edmund Something and he had the bluest eyes I've ever seen. He also, to my delight, had decided that I was one of the People He Needed to Impress. "Hello, Sydney! How was your wedding?"

"Grand," I said, sliding past him to the small alcove behind Reception that constitutes my domain. A big calendar, a medium-sized rolltop desk, and a chair that keeps getting pinched every time I'm not actually sitting on it. It's a small empire, but everyone has to start somewhere. "No one got upset, no one had a meltdown, we'll count it as a victory."

He put his head to one side, a studied motion: someone had probably told him he looked particularly darling that way. "Your boyfriend called," he said.

"On the inn's phone?" That wasn't normal; Ali always calls me directly.

"Well, not your *boyfriend* exactly," Edmund said. I was clearly going to have to shake some sense into this one. "His name is Zack, and he sounds divine."

"He's my landlord," I said sourly, "and there's nothing divine about him."

"Better and better," said Edmund. "I like a bad boy as much as the next guy."

I wrestled my chair from beside the copier and sat down on it. I'd forgotten to turn my phone back on after the wedding; sure enough, he'd called me there too. I sighed and pressed voicemail. "Sydney, hey, hi, it's Zack. I'm just wondering what's going on across the street." Of course he was; everyone in this town loves to gossip. "The police have been here, and a van from the—" he lowered his voice, possibly to show some sort of hushed respect—"coroner's office. So you have to tell me, Sydney, is Mrs. Mattos all right? And if she is, is she one of those crazy ladies who murders people and puts them in her *cellar*?"

He sounded thrilled by the idea. "Call me back, love, and tell me *everything*!"

I wasn't about to tell him anything, much less everything. Knowing Zack, once he heard about a skeleton in the wall, he'd immediately create a Haunted Night at the nightclub and make expensive over-the-top spooky cocktails with dry ice.

But thus reminded, I gave Julie a call. "I hear our friend in the wall was taken away," I said.

"He's gone to the medical examiner's," she said.

"He? It's a man?"

"A manner of speech," she said dismissively.

"So when will you find out?" I was feeling oddly attached to this corpse. Or skeleton. Or "remains," as Julie had called it.

A sigh. "Sydney, it's a process," she said. "A forensic anthropologist will be able to do a biological profile to identify the person. That's age, gender, ancestry, all that. The medical examiner could possibly make an identification through dental records."

Dental records always sounded like an awkward proposition to me. I had an image of someone sending out a notice to every dentist in the world, asking if an x-ray might be in their files. There had to be some more sophisticated way they did it.

Julie was still talking. "The anthropologist can do a facial reconstruction," she said. "But no matter what they find, you still have to ask yourself the question: if someone was living in that house when the body was put into the wall, there would have been a horrible smell as it decomposed," she said. "Unless the house wasn't occupied."

"Small chance of that," I muttered. "The Mattos family hasbeen there forever. They're Portuguese, not nouveau riche. You ever hear of one of their houses standing empty?"

"No," she admitted. "Someone was there."

"Someone was there," I agreed.

"Then there's the psychotic killer option," Julie went on, connecting with some knowledge base I didn't know much about. "Psychotic killers will sometimes keep their victims close by so they can visit them. Maybe that was what happened here."

I honestly couldn't imagine Mrs. Mattos keeping a victim close so she could visit it. Or having a victim in the first place. Blood didn't go with her color scheme. It just baffled me.

"Of course, there's another possibility," said Julie. "Maybe not so much anymore, but in the past, people sometimes found—or stole—human bones and kept them for curiosity's sake. Or there were skeletons or skulls looted from cemeteries for some sort of ritual." She paused. "Of course, most commonly, they were brought home by servicemen returning from conflict areas like Vietnam. That would make it easier."

"It would?"

"There are ways to identify a trophy skull," she said. "Also, if the skull has a calvarium cut, it would point to there having been an autopsy. There's some evidence that in New England, people sometimes exhumed their loved ones to have them close by."

"You're making this up," I protested.

"Not at all." Then she relented. "Okay, so I just learned it all myself. But it's pretty interesting."

"Was there that cal-something cut on this skull?" She had, after all, looked at it a lot more closely than I had.

"No," she admitted. "But that doesn't mean an exhumation didn't happen. Just that the body hadn't been autopsied."

I sighed. "Well, that might make more sense than somebody getting walled up and then decomposing close by where other people are living. The smell must have been horrible." A sudden thought occurred. "Julie— they were dead, weren't they, when they went into the wall? They weren't walled up alive and left to die there, right?"

"That," she said, and her voice was as distant as the sea, "remains to be seen."

5

"You are not a detective." I didn't realize I'd said it out loud until Edmund turned around from the front desk. "What was that, love?"

"Just talking to myself." *You are not a detective. You have other things to deal with. Do not think about this skeleton, do not think about Mrs. Mattos, and start thinking about your own life. Just breathe, Riley.*

My own life included my far-too-neglected boyfriend. I hadn't heard from Ali since he'd told me that hijab wasn't the same as a headscarf. That wasn't unusual; we often went for days and occasionally for weeks without speaking due to his job, which necessitated undercover work. "Not deep undercover," he told me once, and to my horror I heard about agents who spent months and even years pretending to be someone else for the sake of a sting.

Marriages didn't last long in ICE's Human Trafficking division.

I had no idea whether the time was convenient for him or not, but I pressed his icon on my smartphone anyway. He could always not answer. "Sydney."

"Hi," I said. "Is this a bad time?"

"Not particularly. Wait just a sec." I heard a door closing, and then he was back. "Okay, we're good. Everything okay?"

I found another body, I wanted to say, but thought he probably wouldn't see the humor in it. Like Julie, Ali thinks there's something a little strange that I seem to attract stray murderous thoughts around myself. Not that Ali hasn't had his share of murderous thoughts *involving* me, in all probability. "Everything's good," I said. "So tell me about Karen."

He sighed. "It's not that she's taking religion seriously that's the problem," he said. "I think that's a good thing, actually. I sometimes wish I were a better Muslim myself. It's this strain of Islam she's going after that has me concerned."

41

Fundamentalism. The word hung between us, unspoken. "You were going to tell me why a hijab isn't a headscarf," I said instead.

"This business of wearing a headscarf isn't Islamic," he said. "This whole stupid modern movement got codified by radical clerics in places any woman would just love to hang out, like Iran, and Saudi Arabia, and Taliban Afghanistan, and the Islamic State. They're the ones who conflated hijab with headscarf." He paused. "In case you're interested, in Arabic the word for headscarf is tarha. Not hijab. Hijab means isolation, it means barriers, it means hiding. If women have to cover themselves to keep men from attacking them, then there's something seriously wrong that doesn't have anything to do with scarves. Talk about blaming the victim."

Ali sees a lot of victim blaming in his line of work.

"Besides, wearing the headscarf—it's an artifact of a patriarchal society. It's about the subjugation of women." He let out his breath. "She can't do that. She's not some backwards cleric's wife in the backstreets of Kabul. She's Boston's frigging police commissioner!"

And his sister. I got that. But still. "You know, for someone who's so supposedly open-minded, you're not wasting any time judging someone else's morals," I observed.

"I'm not judging anyone," Ali said angrily. "I'm just saying—"

"Bullshit you aren't," I said, interrupting him. "You think progressive values are the only ones that count. You're fine as long as the values you're defending are your own."

Wait. Were we actually having a *fight*?

"This isn't who my family is. Lebanon's a progressive country," he said. "We come from Beirut, not Riyadh or Tehran. Everything our parents stood for, education, culture, everything we ever learned or believed goes against wearing a headscarf."

"Maybe, but Karen has the right to make her own decisions about how she wants to live, doesn't she? She's making a choice about how to present herself to the world, her values. Isn't that the point of a progressive society?"

"Not if doing it hurts other people."

"Who, *you*? Is that it? You're saying it hurts *you* somehow? You're angry because she's not as progressive as you are and you're thinking about how that reflects on *you*?"

Yeah: we were having a fight. Edmund was openly eavesdropping.

"Of course not. It's about other women, it hurts other women, women everywhere,

43

women who're told they're worthless and taught that they're men's possessions, which is a first step down a slippery slope to complete gender servitude. I see it every day in my work, and frankly I don't see how you of all people can support that!"

Oh, yeah. *Major* fight.

I took a deep breath. "I believe people should be able to make choices is all," I said. "Even bad ones. Even destructive ones."

"Even ones," he said, his voice dangerous, "that hurt other people."

Back to that. And he had me there. "Knowingly," I said. "Not when they *know* they're hurting other people. But sometimes you hurt somebody without knowing it. Without realizing what you're doing, without thinking through all the possible repercussions. I don't think Karen's out to destroy the sisterhood or anything. She might just not have thought it all the way through."

"She has a PhD. You can't say she can't think things through."

"It's in criminal justice, for heaven's sake, Ali! Not philosophy. Not religion."

"It's a life decision," he said stubbornly. "Of course she's thought it all the way through. She thought it through and then she made the wrong decision." He paused. "Don't you see? Everything she does has meaning. Every decision she makes impacts hundreds of other lives. Karen's a frigging role model. Police cadets look at her and see who they want to become some day. And now they'll see a woman subservient to a crazy man's interpretation of religion that isn't even part of that religion at all, but who knows that with crazies running around telling the world that this is what it means to be a Muslim! She's sending all the wrong messages, and I *just don't get it.*"

There it was: that last bit, the puzzlement in his voice. Ali and Karen had always been close, and now they weren't. It wasn't just his untold numbers of women and cadets she was hurting: it was him, it was her brother. The political is always personal. "Maybe she'll change her mind," I said gently.

"I don't even know how to talk to her," he said, baffled. "I don't know her, I don't know who she is, not anymore."

"It'll be all right." But I didn't see how, and the phrase sounded ridiculously inadequate as well as untruthful.

"Yes," he said. He clearly didn't want to fight anymore. He didn't want to pursue it. He sounded exhausted. "Ali—"

"It's all right. Listen, Sydney, I have to go."

"Ali—"

"We'll talk later," he said, and disconnected.

And I hadn't even told him about the skeleton yet. Another conversation I wasn't looking forward to. But he wasn't the only one who needed to get back to work. I sighed and pulled out my daybook and started writing up the wedding.

Even as I was writing, though, what I was seeing was Karen's face, and I wondered what she looked like with her beautiful dark glossy hair imprisoned, and what color head covering went with a commissioner's uniform.

***

Mike, the Race Point Inn's manager, called a staff meeting the next day.

These meetings were a new venture, the direct result of Mike's unfortunate obsession with self-improvement during the off-season. He took adult education classes in Orleans and Harwich, and we could all tell which one was on by his sudden enthusiasms that generally rocked the inn for a time and then subsided as reality forced its way back into our lives. Once it had been a Shakespeare course, and we gave up the dining room to a production of Antony and Cleopatra before discovering that, in terms of being a theatre company, we were actually an excellent inn. Another time he'd done accounting for dummies and tried to revamp the whole bookkeeping system.

This past winter's course had to do with leadership, hence his insistence upon periodic staff meetings. Attendance was spotty, due partly to the demands of actually running an inn, and partly to Adrienne, our diva chef, who refused to leave her kitchen or, indeed, talk to anyone but the maître d' or Glenn the owner.

We met in the main dining room, with coffee and midmorning carbs created by Angus, the pastry chef, second in command to Adrienne and in attendance at the meeting representing the kitchen. I looked around the table: Mike, Glenn, Edmund, Angus, Beatriz (head housekeeper), Martin (the aforementioned maître d'), Philip (in charge of all alcohol and bartenders), and *moi*. Not for the first time, I contemplated what a masculine enclave the Race Point Inn was.

"All right," said Mike briskly. "First thing: we're less than three weeks off from the Portuguese Festival. What do we have going?"

We all shifted in our chairs and tried not to catch anybody's eye. Angus finally cleared his throat. "Adrienne's got a prix-fixe Portuguese-inspired dinner on for the whole week," he said.

"Good," said Mike, nodding. "Sydney?"

I was startled. "What? I don't have any Portuguese-themed weddings, if that's what you're asking."

"Other events?"

"We've got the fado concert in the restaurant that Thursday," Martin reminded me smoothly. "And we're hosting Bishop Moreira da Cunha for a luncheon after the Blessing of the Fleet on Sunday." I made a face at him: Martin likes to show off. He'd probably been practicing pronouncing the bishop's Portuguese name for days.

"Good, good." Mike liked events like those; we got a lot of publicity mileage out of them for relatively little extra outlay.

The Portuguese Festival is held in Provincetown every year in June, parts of it noisy and raucous, parts of it celebratory and even solemn. People come from all the other Portuguese enclaves, Fall River and New Bedford and Gloucester, all the places where the Azorean sailors and fishermen settled, and the town explodes with music and smells like a bakery the whole week. It's joyous and boisterous and a lot of fun. At the end of the week, on Sunday, all the boats in the fishing fleet—now seriously depleted at around fifty-five boats, but still there and still functional—are vividly decorated and motor past the end of the pier in a boat parade, while the bishop solemnly blesses them for the upcoming year.

I've seen some of the pictures these guys take of the high seas out on Stellwagen and Georges Bank: they need all the blessings they can get.

Glenn said, "Where is he staying? The bishop?" Wisely, he decided not to attempt the name.

"He doesn't stay," said Mike. "He comes down in the morning, says Mass at Saint Peter's, does the procession, gets on the *Province-town II* ferry for the Blessing, has lunch, and leaves." Glenn inherited the inn when his partner Barry, the inn's former owner, was killed; he was still catching up.

Angus was peering at his watch. Beatriz, who is Portuguese but hadn't said a word about the Festival (she let the Americans, as she called anyone who wasn't Portuguese, all thrash out the plans; all she cared about was getting to go eat under the tent that was set up in the Bas Relief Park and listen to middle-aged Portuguese crooners sing middle-aged Portuguese songs) was also looking faintly irritated. "All right," said Mike. "Thanks for coming, everybody. Let's make it the best Festival ever!"

Wow. With a pep talk like that, how could we go wrong?

6

And so Provincetown got ready for the
Portuguese Festival.

The story was that one fine spring day in
1947 two Provincetown fishermen made a
visit to the port of Gloucester up on the
North Shore (off-Cape, which is really something of a big deal) for that city's annual
Blessing of the Fishing Fleet celebration, a
tradition said to honor and help protect New
England men whose lives were dependent on
the sea. Inspired by their trip, they brought
the Festival tradition back to Provincetown
with them, and a trap boat called the Harbor
Bar—the captain was a Rego—was the first

boat to be blessed, resulting in (of course) a record earning that year.

It didn't expand into becoming the Portuguese Festival until the 1990s, and now the Festival had become a tradition of traditions. Everyone talks about there being a rift between the Portuguese fishing community and the artist community, but when the Festival started—and still today, to some extent— there was an overlap. While there were differences among various segments of the community—East End and West End, Azorean and Lisboan families, captains and crews, fishermen and artists—everyone was there for each other when necessary. Fishermen fed artists; artists painted fishermen.

The Blessing of the Fleet was the official start of the summer season, and the fishermen haul, paint, repair, and decorate their boats for the festivities. It's a reminder, one that might be more and more important, of a vital way of life that is still going on, strong despite the setbacks, often behind the scenes. Tourists walk down MacMillan and they glance at the draggers, the scallop and lobster boats, and they if they notice them at all, it's to consider them picturesque. But the men— and, once in a while, a woman—who work these boats are here year in and year out, swinging a hammer in January to pay the bills, doing engine repair, waiting to get back out there. And then they're out for days and days, in every weather imaginable, and nearly all of Provincetown's product is consumed on-Cape. And people still will ask a waiter if the fish is fresh.

One of my favorite Portuguese Festival traditions is the carrying of banners with the names of the boats. Most of them are boats that exist only in memory now, parts of the fleet lost at sea, a way of life that's all but disappeared. But the banners aren't about nostalgia; they're about pride.

In the old days, the Festival included even more activities: the greasy pole that you can still see at Saint Peter's Fiesta in Gloucester, and what people talked about, mostly, were the dory races between the piers that used to precede the Blessing. But even without all that, the Festival is still one of the best, most joyous, and most inclusive events in Provincetown.

On a gloriously beautiful morning, when I'd started the day with a walk on the town beach and marveled at the colors of the sea and sky—why live here, after all, if you can't enjoy the same things that draw the tourists?—Mrs. Mattos called.

"Sydney? Is that you?" Mrs. Mattos doesn't trust telephones to actually work; she raises her voice to a level that makes the cell towers redundant.

"It's me, Mrs. Mattos." As you phoned me, that actually makes sense.

"Come for dinner tonight." It was an order, not an invitation, but why not? It had been a week since they'd taken the witch-cat and the skeletonized remains out of her house. Maybe there was news. "I'd love to, Mrs. Mattos, thank you."

She said something that sounded a lot like "humph," and hung up. Not for Mrs. Mattos the convenience of a cell phone; she'd only relatively recently upgraded her landline from its earlier rotary incarnation. There's something very satisfying about hanging up the phone that you just don't get when you press the little red dot on a smartphone. I almost envied her.

Almost.

Julie hadn't called, but I suspected that she had more pressing items on her plate than a probably-archaeological-artifact that had spent the past 50 years—at least—in someone's wall. Even as the town is flooded with holidaymakers, so too does the police department have to contend with *its* annual wave of seasonal baby police officers to train. (I am not kidding. They all look about thirteen. And they get to carry *guns*.)

Still, I'd given the whole thing some thought. And research. There was, apparently, a whole academic discipline devoted to hidden charms and the magical protection of buildings. It even had an official-sounding name: *apotropaios* (a Greek word that, appropriately enough, means the turning away of evil).

There was, I read, direct evidence that witch-bottles were used to counter witchcraft, and written charms seem to have protected against all manner of supernatural dangers. The evidence for concealed shoes, horse skulls, dried cats and ritual protection marks is based entirely on physical evidence rather than writings, but it seems that with these we had the same broad intention: protection from harm.

Why shoes? There was a decent answer: it's the only thing people wear that keeps the shape (and some would say the personality and even the essence) of the person who had worn it. Children's shoes were especially popular because of their presumed innocence (though I'd met a couple of kids here on vacation who'd have you believing in Damien in a heartbeat); they made for an especially protective atmosphere. Personally, I wouldn't want to put them on the front lines of battle against evil, but what did I know?

They didn't even have to be in walls, apparently; that just made it easier to clean around them. There were examples from rural places where old shoes were left on a stool outside a house or even apartment to keep out intruders.

I doubted that Zack would like me starting that particular practice.

And shoes are, apparently, everywhere. They've been found in the walls of houses, museums, schools, shops, and pubs; even churches—England's Ely Cathedral and Winchester Cathedral have some. All of them had been worn, and even worn out (probably some thrifty homemaker wanting to get every bit of use out of the shoes before they went on to their next life), none of them matched, and all of them were in walls or attics. Evil, presumably, was free to come in through the cellar.

The other element I found fascinating was the secrecy. Apparently that's a hallmark of magic practices, that secrecy; often the people living in a given place a generation or more after the object's placement didn't know it was there. I conjured up images of lanterns casting yellow light at midnight, furtive shadows, a quick sealing off of the hole made to accommodate the shoes.

Or the cat.

Cats were powerful anti-witch tools. Well, they apparently worked: I hadn't seen any witches around Mrs. Mattos' house at all. These cats obviously weren't dried when they were concealed and it strikes me that this would have been a fairly significant act on the concealer's behalf. Clearly there was some strong notion that hiding the animal would serve a purpose, which was almost certainly some kind of protective magic. Poor cats. They hunt vermin in life and apparently performed so well that they were tasked with doing it on a spiritual plane after death.

None of what I'd read, however, pointed to a reason why a *person* would be sharing their afterlife location with a cat. Sure, there were cultures that practiced something called foundation sacrifices, during which an animal or even a human would be killed and placed in the foundation to appease the gods or protect the place, but they weren't in North America and they predated Mrs. Mattos' house by a few hundred centuries.

I still had a feeling that she knew more about this than she was saying, and dinner was going to present a perfect opportunity to find out what.

***

I dressed for dinner.

Nothing formal—P'town is notoriously *in*formal—but better than my jeans and Provincetown Library t-shirt, anyway. A light summery dress, no tights, just slid my feet into sandals, a comb though my tangles, and voila: Almost-Presentable Sydney.

I brought a bottle of wine, too. French, not Portuguese. There are some places where you just have to draw the line.

If you didn't know, you'd never have thought that there had ever been a hole in the wall. Mrs. Mattos sat me down in the same chintz-covered chair as before, with a metal TV tray beside me (they still *make* those things?) and gave me a glass of sweet port. "You got it fixed," I said, gesturing toward the wall. Sydney Riley, master of the obvious.

She perched on the edge of the sofa. "Couldn't be thinking about that cat," she said. "Walked right upstairs and into my dreams, it did. Better off walled up again. Drink your port."

I obediently took a sip. I've had better tasting cough syrup. "The police didn't mind?"

"Haven't heard a word from them," she said virtuously and probably untruthfully, then spoiled the effect by adding, "And no one's going to tell me what to do in my own house, anyways."

"I see. And the cat…?"

"Still there." Her voice was grim. "I figured he'd been doing his job all along, he can keep doing it for a while."

Sounded sensible to me. I wondered, though, if any of Julie's minions had cleared the space completely before Mrs. Mattos had it filled back in. We'd gone along in a progression: shoes, cat, person. Who knew what might be next?

"So," I said, as though picking up the discarded threads of an earlier conversation, "how long have you lived in this house, Mrs. Mattos?" Can't fault me for not getting straight to the point.

She downed her port as though she were doing tequila shots at the Old Colony Tap, P'town's dive bar. "Ever since I was married," she said grimly. I thought about it. Marriage as prison term?

"And when was that?"

She hesitated, and for a moment I didn't think she'd answer. Maybe she was doing math in her head. Figuring out the last time the house had been remodeled. "Sixty-five years this July," she said.

Wow. A lot could happen in sixty-five years, which was roughly twice my age. "And your husband? He lived here before that, didn't he?"

"It's a big house," she said. "His father were alive then, we all lived here together."

I had no idea how to ask what I wanted to know. Did someone disappear somewhere in there? Was there an argument? Anybody get—um—killed? Just a tad obvious.

She stood up. "You finish that port, so we can eat," she said, and headed back into the kitchen. I looked around a little wildly for a plant where I could dump it, but Mrs. Mattos clearly didn't have time for such frivolity as indoor plants in her life. I swallowed the port as quickly as I could and trailed after her. "Can I help?"

"Why? I look like I need help?"

Okay. I backed off. "Can I open the wine?" Anything to make sure there was no more port in my future.

She flapped her hands in the direction of the Châteauneuf-du-Pape. "Go ahead. I've got to get this roast out anyways."

She'd set the table in a dismally dark dining room. I found wine glasses and poured, and stopped myself from offering again to help as she laboriously brought dishes to the table: the roast itself, broccoli, mashed potatoes, bread. Finally we were sitting and she was making sure that there was enough food on my plate to sink a battleship. "You don't eat enough to keep a fly alive."

"I'm fine. This is all lovely." I took a first tentative sip of wine. Yes: much, much better. "So are you doing all right?" I asked. "I know that all this must have been really upsetting, finding—um—all that in your wall. Since you've lived here for so long, and your husband's family before you."

"They's the ones built it," she said, surprisingly. I waited while she took a bite, chewed, swallowed. "Back in 1835."

"Were they all fishermen?"

She gave me a look that seemed to seriously question my sanity and didn't bother answering. What else would they be?

I tried again. "Mrs. Mattos, if the house has always been in the family, then it had to be someone in the family who put the cat in." Never mind the person; we'd get to that. Start small.

"Don't you think I know that?" She shook her head; the American education system was not living up to expectations. It had taken me this long to figure *that* out?

"So do you know who it was?"

She took a swallow of wine that was anything but genteel, and swallowed. "No," she said. Uncompromising.

I didn't believe her for a second.

"There's cake for after," she said, encouragingly. Back on safer ground. Did she really think I was going to go there?

I put my elbows on the table. "Mrs. Mattos, you know I'm just asking the questions the police will ask."

She shook her head. "Not if it's—archae-something. Not if it's over a hunnert years old."

"They'll still want to know." I had no idea if this was true or not, but for sure *I* wanted to know. This had to be a Mattos—well, that, or someone who someone named Mattos didn't like.

But I still couldn't get away from wondering about the smell.

Mrs. Mattos had other fish to fry. "Anyway, I got the insulation in," she said. "No more workmen in the house." That seemed to represent a bigger relief than getting the remains out of there.

"Congratulations." I put my fork down. "Now tell me."

"Nothing to say."

"I am sitting here until you tell me," I said. "I'm going to be really hard to vacuum around."

She looked vaguely shocked. "You can't be staying here."

"Then tell me."

Mrs. Mattos shook her head, heaved a big theatrical sigh. "We had some work done after the war," she said. "Maybe a lot after it. When them flower children was all over the place. Added the bathroom onto the back of the house. Coulda been done then."

I stared at her. "You had the bathroom put onto the back and you didn't notice them doing anything in the parlor?"

"I wasn't here, though, was I? Can't be expected to keep a clean house with all that dust and noise around. Joe and me, we went to stay with his cousin."

"Which one?" Did I mention how many people in town are called Mattos?

She shrugged. "Don't matter. Three weeks, we had to stay there, and when we got back, I had to strip and wax the kitchen floor again, they made such a terrible mess."

Three weeks. I wondered how long it took for a body to decompose, to stop smelling like... well, a *body*. I'd have to ask Julie. Whether or not she'd tell me was anybody's guess. "But the bathroom looked good?"

"What?"

"The bathroom," I said. "The addition. You were happy with it?"

A faint smile. "You gotta know, if you spend years going to the outhouse at the back of the house, any bathroom's a miracle."

I could imagine that for sure. "And that's the only time someone could have put... the cat... in the wall? What about vacations?"

She had that look of incredulity on her face again. "What do you think, we're tourists? Think we're rich? We never went on vacation. In my time, people didn't do that."

At least not people who made their living from the sea, I thought. Another point for Miss Insensitive. "So that was the only time," I said again.

She didn't want to agree with me. "Are you finished with that?"

I nodded. "It was delicious."

"Don't lie to me. You have no appetite."

"I can't eat when I'm solving a crime," I objected. "And you *could* make it easier for me."

She put down her fork. "What is it that you want from me?" she demanded. "That I know who this man is? That he is some cousin? That there was an argument that couldn't be settled? I can't tell you that. I don't know who this man is!"

"Or woman," I said. "It could have been a woman."

"Of course not. It couldn't have—" She stopped.

I stared at her. She could have been clearer if a neon light bulb had come on over her head, but only marginally. "You know," I said.

She stood up, picked up the plates. "Nothing," she said shortly. "No one."

I followed her into the kitchen. "If you know, you have to tell the police," I said. She turned on the faucet, and I raised my voice so she could hear me over it. "It's a woman, isn't it, Mrs. Mattos? Mrs. Mattos?"

***

"It's a woman," said Julie.

We were standing in the driveway of the police station. The weather had turned unexpectedly hot and I could feel the heat trapped in the concrete rising up through my feet. "She knows who it is," I said.

"Emilia Mattos?"

I nodded. "Her husband's great-grandfather built the house," I said. "There's no way that anything happened there without the family knowing about it."

"I don't know," said Julie. She wasn't looking at me. She was facing the street and her eyes were automatically checking out every vehicle driving past. Cop's eyes. "Report says it's old. Not *archaeological*-old, but about fifty years old."

"So what? You have an idea how old Mrs. Mattos is?" I changed tack. "Besides, I'm telling you, she knows who it is. They had a bathroom put in and the house was empty for three weeks." I paused. "Is that enough time for the smell to go away?"

She sighed. Educating me isn't on Julie's list of favorite ways to spend her time. "It was in a dry place," she began.

"You're kidding, right?" I stared at her until she looked at me instead of out at the street. "Julie, we're sticking out into the Atlantic Ocean, in case you hadn't noticed."

"The house isn't on the water," she said. "And it was dry. The cat was mummified, remember, and it's possible that the body went through the decomposition stages fairly quickly. It releases certain substances—"

I held up my hand "TMI," I said. I don't need to know about the substances bodies release. "Mrs. Mattos said the construction happened when there were flower-children all over town, so that means sometime in the 1960s or seventies, right? And that corresponds to your forensic people's estimation?"

"More or less," she said guardedly. The police don't like you telling them how to do their jobs.

It wasn't going to deter me. "So all you have to do is look for missing persons around that time." Really, this crime solving wasn't all that difficult.

"Jesus," she said. "What do you think, they entered information into a database that I can just call up now? Do you know how many tourists come here every year? Do you know how many of them in the sixties and seventies were runaways? Everyone was dropping out of school, doing drugs, protesting the war in Vietnam."

I looked at her speculatively, and she shook her head. "No, I wasn't here then. I was just about *born* then."

"But you know your history."

"I know my *town*."

There was a pause. "Anyway," she started to say, and I interrupted. "Then ask Mrs. Mattos."

"Gee whiz, Sherlock, I would never have thought of that! Good thing you're here to give me advice."

No, I decided: people in law enforcement definitely don't want you telling them how to do their jobs. "Okay, fine," I said. "I have weddings to work on, anyway."

She caught my arm as I was turning away. "There's just one thing," she said. "But I don't want you to say anything to Emilia about it."

"What is it?"

Another sharp glance at the street in case someone was doing something untoward on Shank Painter Road. "The skeleton wasn't alone."

"No," I agreed, puzzled. "There was a cat there, too."

"Cats don't make people kill other people and put their bodies in walls," she said. She obviously hadn't read her Poe. "But babies do."

I stared at her. "She was pregnant," I said slowly.

Julie cleared her throat. "She was pregnant," she agreed. "And if you think Emilia Mattos doesn't know exactly who in Provincetown got pregnant and when, you haven't the faintest idea of what the culture is like in this town, you're only kidding yourself."

"It's a motive," I said, and she gave me another of her gee-whiz-Sherlock looks. "I think that's a reasonable hypothesis," she said. "Someone got pregnant sometime in the late sixties or early seventies, and someone else wanted to make sure that baby never saw the light of day."

7

Mike was sitting on the inn's front porch when I got back. He never does that. He sits in his office or strides around the inn being his version of fierce.

I stopped on the top stair and looked at him. "If you're waiting for the parade," I said, "it doesn't happen until the festival actually begins."

He grinned amiably. "Just enjoying the sun."

I took the rattan chair next to his. "It is nice," I agreed. We'd had a lot of rain in the spring, and if you live in a tourist town, that's worrisome. People don't go to the beach in the rain. They cancel inn reservations. They go back from whence they came. The sun is our friend.

We sat for a few moments savoring it together. Mike finally spoke. "How is your handsome boyfriend?"

Ali gets more than his share of stares in Provincetown, where gay men outnumber straight ones by some ridiculous percentage. He deserves the stares, of course: I'm not the only one who thinks he's gorgeous. He is clearly Middle Eastern, very exotic, with his dark eyes and olive skin. "Family troubles," I said.

"Oh, dear. I know what those can be like."

I looked at him curiously. "You never talk about your family," I observed.

"You noticed? Clever girl."

"The aforementioned family troubles?"

He nodded. "The aforementioned indeed." He sighed. "I grew up here, you know. In P'town."

"I didn't know."

"My family used to own one of the candy joints on Lopes Square," Mike said. "We lived over the store. Always smelled like chocolate."

I smiled. "Then it can't have been all bad."

"We used to play on the town beaches, screaming and shouting," he said. "Me and my cousins, they always got shipped here for the summer. We turned tan overnight and didn't put our shoes on until September."

"It sounds idyllic."

He nodded, his eyes on some distant past. "Maybe it was." Suddenly he grinned. "I remember once we were down on the town beach in the East End and doing something, raising holy hell, and this big guy came out on his deck and yelled down at us kids to shut the hell up." He looked at me. "It was Norman Mailer."

I smiled again. "It seems everyone who's lived in town for a while has a Norman Mailer story," I said. And it was true: Mailer was a *force majeure* throughout the sixty years he maintained a summer residence here. He'd get drunk in a bar and invite the local Portuguese fishermen to step outside to settle their differences (and they did). He brought Jackie Kennedy to visit because he and Gore Vidal had told her it was the "wild west of the east." He lost arm-wrestling matches to someone who was rather delightfully called Bottles Sousa. He wrote lyrically of the town and the people who lived in it, and I don't think that in all the years since he died, with all the other

writers who have since then called Provincetown home, there is anyone who can hold a
candle to him. The fact that everyone still tells
Norman Mailer stories says it all.

Mike was considering the remark. "I
guess that's true," he said after a moment.
"What a place this must have been then, back
in the sixties and seventies."

And then it hit me. She had lived here
then, the mysterious girl with the big bad secret who had ended up in Emilia Mattos' wall
for half a century. She'd been pregnant when
she was put there, so she had to be young,
and probably enjoying the kind of bohemian
lifestyle that Norman Mailer wrote about so
eloquently. What had she done, who had she
crossed, so that she wasn't here in Provincetown getting old and telling tales of the past?

"You were here then," I said to Mike.
"What was it like?"

"Give me a break, I was born in 1980,"
he said. "And by the time I was twenty, I
couldn't wait to get out. I thought the place
was provincial." He grinned, suddenly, vividly. "Here's something you won't believe.
Odd as it seems, I couldn't come out in
P'town," he said. "I know, I know, lots of
people come here to do that. People used to
come here from all over the world to feel free
to be gay, to walk down the street holding

hands. But everyone here—everyone in town knew me as little Mikey. I had to go to New York to figure all that stuff out."

"But you came back."

"Yeah." He thought for a moment. "It's home. It's just that sometimes—well, maybe it's that you can't learn about yourself at home. You have to go somewhere else, be challenged, learn to stand up for something, some principle or some person, to really start feeling comfortable in your skin. Once you've done that, then home can work again."

It sounded deep. "I'm not so sure about that," I said. "My mother's always on me about moving back home. I can't imagine anything worse." And that was true: my mother is excruciating even at a distance. Any closer and I'd have to kill her.

"See? We all have family troubles."

"I suppose so." I sighed. We sat quietly looking out at Commercial Street going by. "So what happened is, Ali's sister's turned ultra-conservative, and he's scared," I said finally.

"For her?"

"I suppose for her," I said. I wasn't really sure. "I think it's a lot of things. Yeah, covering her head's bound to make her even more enemies at work, and she has enough of them already, people who resent her because she's a woman, people who resent her because she's young and smart, and now people will resent her because she's putting her religion out there. But he also—I guess he mistrusts it, you know? The whole conversion to fundamentalism. I mean, she was only in Lebanon for two weeks, and she comes back totally different? What's not to mistrust?"

He nodded. "What do you think?"

"I don't even know what I think," I said. "You should've heard us on the phone. One of us was defending her and the other one was talking about feminism. And you'd never have guessed which of us was which in the conversation. And I just think—" I broke off as Mike's phone started playing Madonna.

Madonna? *Really?* He grimaced and fished it out of his pocket, glancing at the called ID and swiping across to answer. "Hey, Glenn."

The inn's owner. You take his calls. I got up and waggled my fingers at Mike and went on into the inn. And spent the rest of the day immersed in weddings.

It is my day job, after all.

8

I gave up on cable television years ago.

That was when my friend John, who's the executive director at WOMR, Provincetown's community radio station and a true lover of gadgets, introduced me to Roku, and after that there was no going back. Instead of paying ridiculous rates for myriad channels I would never watch, I now had tidy little subscriptions to Netflix and Amazon Prime video, and I was quite happy with that.

Which was why I was curled up that evening with a glass of wine, my cat purring beside me, and the English detective series *Luther* on the TV, when the telephone rang. I don't have a Madonna ringtone; my musical taste runs more to Aerosmith. And I know how old that makes me sound.

It was Mirela. I hit pause and answered. "What's up?"

She came right to the point. "When were you going to tell me?" she demanded.

"Tell you what?"

"That there was something else in Mrs. Mattos' wall. I tell you so much information about the witches and the shoes and then there is a cat and a skeleton and you want to keep that all for yourself?"

I snuggled in deeper with Ibsen, who opened his eyes briefly as he accommodated me. This was clearly going to be a long conversation. The delectable Idris Elba on the television was going to have to wait. "I haven't seen you since it happened," I pointed out.

"What is in your hand?"

"Excuse me?"

"This thing you are holding," she said. "It is called a telephone. You can call. You *should* call."

"I assumed," I said, "that you'd know about it already." Mirela has the best gossip pipeline in town.

"You can make up for it now," she said. "Tell me everything."

I sighed. "So it's a female. Probably young. Mrs. Mattos has been living in that house since she got married, which was sometime in the Dark Ages, and she remembers one time when they did some construction and she had to go stay elsewhere, so that has to be when the girl got walled up. Mrs. Mattos notices new specks of dust; she really couldn't miss the wall being opened up and somebody's body shoved inside."

"Unless," said Mirela, "she was the one who helped shove it in."

Whoa. That possibility hadn't even crossed my mind. Mrs. Mattos as murderer? "She wouldn't," I said. "Good grief, Mirela, for one thing, she wouldn't kill anybody. She just wouldn't. And for another thing, she'd never let them stay in her wall. She's Catholic—not like I'm Catholic, she's *really* Catholic. She'd insist on a decent burial in hallowed ground, or something like that."

"It might not have been her decision to make," said Mirela.

"What? You think that she'd allow something that awful to happen and then just play cleanup behind it?"

"She is of an age and a culture that would make that possible," said Mirela primly. "The Portuguese women just took care of men's messes back then. And it might not have been murder, sunshine. At the end of the day, it might have been an unfortunate accident."

Unfortunate *accident?* "I don't think so," I said. "She was pregnant."

"Mrs. Mattos?"

"The girl in the wall," I said.

There was a silence, which is completely out of character for Mirela. "So," she said at last.

"So," I agreed.

"An inconvenient pregnancy." She drew in a breath. "When did this construction happen?"

"I think sometime in the early seventies," I said. "Julie says that the skeleton is about fifty years old, give or take a decade."

"I see." Another pause. "What are you going to do about it?"

"What do you mean, what am I going to do about it?" On the TV screen in front of me, Idris Elba was about to put his fist through a wall, and I found myself wondering what was inside it. Why is it that when something bizarre or unexpected happens in your life, then everything else seems to be about that thing? I broke a tooth in the winter and all I saw after that were ads for toothpaste, and everyone seemed to be talking about dentists.

"You are, of course, going to find out what happened," said Mirela. It wasn't a question. "And to whom."

Here we went again. "I am not a detective," I said.

"But you are curious, and you are good at it. And you *know* you want to know."

Well, there was that. Sometime in a heady post-Summer-of-Love Provincetown, a young woman had lived and, presumably, loved, and she hadn't gotten any further along in life. It was a haunting image for sure. "Maybe there's no way to find out," I said, playing devil's advocate. "Provincetown was full of people from everywhere. Runaways, hitchhikers, you name it. That's when the lady in the dunes was found, wasn't it?"

"The lady in the dunes?"

"Out in the Seashore," I said impatiently. "They only ever found parts of her, her hands were gone, most of her teeth. They never found out who she was."

"Well, she wasn't in the wall at the Mattos' house," said Mirela drily.

"And then there were those girls who got killed and buried in Truro," I said. "A local guy picked them up and killed them and buried them. They were from off-Cape, too."

"And *they* weren't in the Mattos' wall, either," said Mirela patiently. "Don't you see, sunshine, this one was personal. This was not a random victim. It's too intimate for that. They knew her, whoever put her in there knew her." She paused. "And all this time, someone thought she was somewhere else."

"How do you figure that?" I gave up and clicked off the TV. Idris would have to survive tonight without me.

"Because no one thought she was in the wall," said Mirela. "There would have been a search. Someone would sometime have remembered something, seen her at the house, anything that might point to what happened. No: they had to make it seem that she had gone somewhere else. So find out who disappeared with a good cover story."

"Mirela, it was the seventies, I keep telling you, the town was full of transients and tourists."

"And she was neither. Why are you fighting this, sunshine?"

Because I don't want to believe that Mrs. Mattos could be part of anything like this. Because Ali is worried about his sister and I'm not giving him enough support. Because it's almost time for the Portuguese Festival and that isn't a time to uncover a tragedy. Because every time there's a body in this town I'm

somehow involved and am going to start being known as Provincetown's answer to Jes-
sica Fletcher. Because I'm a wedding
coordinator and not a detective. "I don't
know," I said.

"If you don't have an answer," said
Mirela, "then that's your answer."

***

So how do you figure out who disappeared unexpectedly? You talk to people who
were there, I thought. Napi Van Derek
seemed a good place to start; his restaurant,
Napi's, is one of my favorites, a fact that
wasn't particularly incidental. If ever you
want to start something new, food should always figure in the early plans. And Napi has
lived in town forever; when he was a kid, people used to come off the ferries—back when
the trip to and from Boston was an elegant
affair, with dinner and dancing—and they'd
toss coins off into the harbor; Napi and his
friends used to dive down off the pier to retrieve and claim them.

A story I didn't really want to dwell on; it
was only last year that I'd gone off that same
pier, in October, trying to get away from
someone who was trying to kill me. Not an
altogether happy memory, though one that

had ended well, as I was still on this mortal coil.

The next evening found me sitting at the bar, a bowl of bouillabaisse and a glass of wine in front of me, and Napi sitting next to me, telling me stories. The stained glass figure above us seemed to be following along. They were great stories. But none of them, it seemed, were getting me any closer to finding out who went missing. With the Portuguese Festival nearly upon us, he was remembering the glory of past festivals, when Provincetown's fishing fleet had been a force to be reckoned with, and the Blessing of the Fleet took over three hours to accomplish, there were so many boats in the harbor. It was all wonderful material, and if I were a writer, I'd have been taking notes.

"There was a girl who went missing," I finally said, recklessly. "Sometime in the 1970s, when you and Helen had your antique shop. Do you remember her?"

He frowned. "Not that I remember."

Not helpful. I tried again. "She probably knew the Mattos family." Big mistake; at the time, about half the town was called Mattos. Okay, so I exaggerate, but still... Napi was shaking his head. "No one that I know," he said.

I had a sinking feeling in my stomach. I was going to have to talk to Mrs. Mattos. I didn't want to talk to Mrs. Mattos. How do you accuse someone of covering up a murder? Because by now I was fairly sure that that was what we were looking at.

Napi had a lot of stories. I wasn't sure he knew about Maria Mattos.

Gail Silva was sitting on the other side of me at the bar and was openly eavesdropping. "I can tell you one," she said. "My father was sailing aboard a Grand Banker, that was this big two-masted ship, and he'd be gone for months at a time. My mother would get word that the vessel was sighted off the back side, and without stopping for anything, she'd grab my hand, and take me down to the beach, where all the other women were gathered. It was always silent; I remember that, the quiet. We waited. When the ship rounded Wood End and the Long Point Light, we watched to see if the boat was coming in at half-mast. That would tell us if anybody's been killed at sea. Then we'd all kneel and bless ourselves and it was such a relief. But if it came in at half-mast it was horrible, because we wouldn't know who it was, who'd been lost at sea, and we had to wait for them to dock to know who was going to do the funeral."

She held up her glass in a mock toast. "Here's to having radios on board," she said.

I raised my glass automatically and hoped my frustration wasn't showing. I finished my wine and my bouillabaisse and thanked Napi and Gail and Dan the bartender, and got myself out of there. I was due to take Mrs. Mattos to the Stop & Shop the next day, and I was running out of excuses.

I walked home from the restaurant, trying to figure out what I needed to know, and who already knew it. The heat had dissipated, as it generally does in the evening, and there was a brisk wind coming in off the water. Commercial Street was jammed with people, people meandering here and there, looking into shop windows, checking out menus, calling to each other. Commercial Street isn't pedestrian-only, but for most of the summer it looks like it is, as sauntering tourists give way only reluctantly (and often belligerently) to the few vehicles that must inch their way forward to get to the bank or the post office.

And there *is* something here for everyone. Drag queens teetering on impossibly high heels. Parents with children in strollers. Gay men strutting their stuff; lesbians holding hands. Bicycles whipping around the pedestrians, carrying summer staff from one job to another.

The flotsam and jetsam of people moving through as though with the tide. In the summertime, it's all about tourism. In the winter, the off-season, Land's End attracts them, the tired, the lonely, even the misfits… but it's all very genteel. There's violence here, but it runs its course behind closed doors or out in the dunes.

We very rarely murder anybody. Though, apparently, if you do decide to knock someone off, it's Sydney Riley, wedding coordinator, who will be investigating. I shook off the feeling of being way over my head and headed home.

Even wannabe detectives get the blues.

9

Someone was in my apartment.

I never lock the door, of course; this is Provincetown. But I also don't expect to come home to find someone in residence— and watching TV, if my ears didn't deceive me. That was enough to slow the sudden thudding of my heart when I'd glanced up and seen the light on. *Breathe, Riley*, I reminded myself, and swung the door open.

Ali was sitting on the loveseat, Ibsen in his lap, both of them intent on the television. He looked up and smiled. "Hey."

"Hey, yourself." I shut the door and leaned against it. "You gave me a heart attack."

"If I were a burglar," he pointed out, "this isn't the place I'd choose to rob. You don't have anything good. I think you're fairly safe."

"There's that," I agreed, and flopped down next to him. Ibsen, disturbed, gave me The Look, stretched, and jumped onto the floor. He likes Ali, for reasons that I don't understand, since Ali persists in calling him The Ib. I put my head on Ali's shoulder. "So what brings you here?"

"I need a reason?" He put his arm around me and kissed my hair.

"A reason? No. A little advance warning; maybe. What if I'd been out all night partying?"

"It would be the first time you'd done it since you were twenty," he said.

"There's that," I said again. Sometimes it feels like I've known Ali my whole life. "So how are things on the home front?"

I felt him shrug. "The same. Karen's not talking to me."

"She has to sometime," I objected. "You live in the same house."

"You'd be amazed at the distances possible inside it," he said.

Jeannette de Beauvoir

I snuggled in deeper. "She'll come around," I said, though I didn't know if I believed it. "And anyway, if it brought you here, there's a silver lining to everything."

He kissed the top of my head again. "Except that's not why I'm here."

Oooh, excellent. He was going to get all mushy and romantic. I love it when he's mushy and romantic. "So why *are* you here?" I asked innocently, waiting to hear something lovely that would make me swoon. Did I mention that Ali writes poetry? This was going to be good.

"I'm on a case," Ali said.

I really need to stop pretending I'm a detective. I clearly can't detect anything. "What?" I sat up, his arm falling off me, and turned to look at him. "You're on a *case*? What case?"

He reached out for me again but I shook him off. "What's going on?"

I'd met Ali when he was on a case. He'd come to Provincetown because he thought my boss, Barry, a beautiful bear of a man, was selling accelerated routes to citizenship via arranged marriages. It turned out to be a great deal more than just that. Barry had ended up dead, and Ali and I had ended up a couple, which meant that now I worried about what he did for a living. There was nothing safe about an ICE case. And now that he was working in Human Trafficking, there was even more to be concerned about. People falsifying green cards is one thing; people buying and selling human beings is in a different league altogether. I loved that he did it, and I hated that he did it, too.

"The Portuguese Festival," he said.

I wasn't in the mood to play word games. That one glass of wine was turning sour in my stomach and the fear that was always there in the background, the fear of someday losing him as I'd lost Barry, was licking around the edges of my consciousness. "What about it?"

"We got some intel—some information," Ali said. He tries hard not to use jargon around me. "There might be a shipment coming in to P'town with the other boats."

A shipment. That was how they all thought about it: a cargo manifest of a product. I shivered. It wasn't all that farfetched an idea as it might sound: the festival takes place as much in the harbor as it does in the town, with pleasure craft, yachts, other fishing vessels all arriving and most of them staying for the week. I didn't know much about how Rex, the harbormaster, took care of registering or whatever he did, and maybe he didn't. But it couldn't be all that difficult to slip in.

Still, Provincetown? "Aren't we small potatoes?" I asked. "If they're using shipping containers, we're way too small for that." But not
too shallow, I reminded myself: Provincetown's the second-largest natural deep harbor
in the world, second only to le Havre in
France.

"No shipping containers," said Ali.
"We've tightened the major ports up. It still
happens, sure, but there's a lot more risk involved. They're bringing them in smaller vessels now, probably transferring out at sea, and
coming in to ports where they're not likely to
be suspicious at a time when a lot of pleasure
shipping's going on. Provincetown's Portuguese Festival. Newport's boat show weeks.
Gloucester's Saint Peter Fiesta. Costs more,
but a much better return on investment."

"And you know for sure they're coming
here?"

He shrugged. "As sure as we can ever
be," he said. He was right. What he played
was still a game of cat and mouse, and the
mice were always finding new ways to evade
the cat. It seemed that every time Ali's department blocked one avenue, three more opened
up. Anyone who thought the era of slaves was
over was deluding themselves: the trade was
alive and well and living in America.

"Way to cast a pall over the party," I said flippantly, but put my head back on his shoulder to show that I wasn't really upset. I wasn't going to make this into a fight over him coming to see me for work or for pleasure; as much as what he does scares me half to death, it's also sexy as hell. Let's face it: I coordinate weddings; he saves lives.

"I know," he said, and hugged me against him. "I'm sorry I'm not here for a better reason."

"Never mind," I said. "I get to see you either way."

He reached for the remote and turned off the TV, which had been on mute anyway. "I have a long day tomorrow," he said, and stretched.

"Is that a hint about going to bed?"

"If you have to ask, I'm doing it wrong."

"No, I said. "You're doing it just right."

***

We had, I decided as I made breakfast, parallel investigations going on. "After all, you need to be talking to people in the Portuguese community, don't you? And so do I. So what we learn can help each other."

"For once," said Ali, pulling his t-shirt on over his head and giving me palpitations as I looked at his chest, "I'm inclined to not be upset about you finding another body."

"Because you're here to protect me?"

"Because whoever she was, she died fifty years ago," he said. "Making Provincetown safe. Chances are, whoever killed her is either dead or too feeble to come after you now." Behind his words, and his eyes, I could see the memory of what had happened last year, when someone *had* come after me.

"So I have your blessing on my endeavor?" I put the two plates of scrambled eggs on the table.

"Let's keep the blessing for the fleet," he said, sitting down. "We'll just say I'm not going to try and talk you out of it this time."

"So what is your plan?" I asked. I don't generally ask Ali about the specifics of his cases—most of the time, I truly wouldn't want to know—but as he was sitting in my apartment I felt it was slightly more appropriate. For meal planning, if nothing else.

"I have a meeting at the Coast Guard station this morning," he said. "Obviously we'd like to stop the shipment before it even makes it to the harbor, but there's some major coordination that's going to have to happen. These eggs are phenomenal, by the way. You have a new technique. How do you make them so fluffy?"

"Gordon Ramsey," I said absently. "I saw it on YouTube." I could just imagine the bureaucratic challenges ahead of Ali. The various branches of the government had never played too well together, a situation the 2016 election had only exacerbated. "Will you be able to? Intercept them at sea, I mean?"

He balanced his hand in a *comme çi, comme ça* gesture. "Maybe. Maybe not. That's why I'm here—for the maybe not part."

"But there's no danger to P'town, is there?" I had sudden visions of ICE agents and slave traders running amok down Commercial Street, staging a shoot-out in front of town hall. "I mean, Ali, the town's going to be full of people." And a whole lot of them were going to be children: various Portuguese dance troupes and musicians came to the Festival from all over New England, marching in the parade, giving performances at various venues in town, staying at the hotels… and almost every group had costumed children as part of the act.

"Not if I can help it."

I put down my fork. "Not if you can help it? That's not exactly reassuring."

Ali looked at me. "You think that there's anything reassuring about what I do?" He held up his hand. "That was a rhetorical question. I can't make any guarantees, Sydney.

Our priority is to keep civilians safe, and I won't risk anybody's life to get these guys. It probably won't even come to that."

I picked up my fork and played with my eggs. "Do you know who the—who they're smuggling in?"

"You mean from where? Probably Albania."

I didn't ask him how he knew. I was too busy pinning a map of the Balkans up in my mind. Didn't Albania have a border with Bulgaria? Maybe Mirela could talk to the girls. I assumed they would be girls. "Is Albania next to Bulgaria?"

"It's next to Greece," said Ali. He was raised in a culture that actually knows something about world geography.

"So is Bulgaria," I said. At least I thought it was.

"A couple of countries between Albania and Bulgaria," said Ali mildly. "Macedonia and Kosovo. But you're close, they're all in the Balkans."

"Oh." I'd thought Kosovo was a city. I was really, really going to have to look at a map one of these days. "Mirela is so going to kick my ass over this when I tell her," I said.

Ali brightened at the mention of her name. He and Mirela have some strange bizarre relationship going. "Now you know, so you don't have to tell her," he said. "What about dinner tonight?"

"What about it?"

"We should take Mirela out somewhere," he said.

"You two have something very weird going on," I pronounced. "But yeah, sure, why not?"

"Good." He stood up and carried his plate to the sink. "What are you doing today?"

"Making calls," I said. That's what I seem to spend a lot of my time doing. "And I have to take Mrs. Mattos grocery shopping this afternoon."

"Mrs. Mattos had better watch out. I sense an opportunity for sleuthing," said Ali.

"You're so marvelously observant." I rinsed both our plates and stacked them in the sink to be dealt with later. Life is too short to spend doing dishes. No dishwasher, of course; my apartment is too small.

I'd kill for a dishwasher.

"That's me, marvelously observant," Ali agreed and drifted off in the direction of the bathroom. I fed Ibsen, grabbed my purse, remembered to comb my hair, and headed over to the inn. Only an hour later than usual, which was pretty good, I thought. Usually

when Ali was there I played hooky more than
I really should.

And we hadn't mentioned his sister once.

10

Ali was right about one thing: it was time to sleuth.

I fetched the Little Green Car from the parking lot where it lived in the summer and pulled up in the street outside the house, leaving the flashers on while I went to get Mrs. Mattos out. This generally takes a while; getting her out the door with her cane and her list and her purse, getting her ensconced in the front seat, dealing with her seatbelt. Fortunately I only inconvenienced one car by making it wait behind me on the narrow street, though he made up for it in his enthusiastic honking and the finger he showed me.

A Connecticut license plate. Of course.

"So," I said, once we were on our way, "The other day you were telling me about having the bathroom built in your house."

"That's the first bathroom," she said. "Later on there was the one for the upstairs, too." Her tone was reverential: this was true luxury.

"And you used an outhouse before that," I said encouragingly.

She was looking out the window. "Carol-Ann wants me to pick up some of that scouring stuff," she said. "It's not on my list."

"I'll add it when we stop," I said. "Do you remember what year that was?"

"What year what was?"

This conversation was going nowhere fast. "When you had the bathroom built," I said, trying to keep my voice from betraying my impatience. "When you had to go stay with your cousin for three weeks." How had she ever fallen for that, anyway? Who takes three weeks to build a bathroom?

"Tony was at summer camp," she said suddenly.

Tony was her son, now middle-aged. He lived in Wellfleet and religiously brought his wife (and, before they grew up and moved out, his two children) for a monthly Sunday dinner at Mrs. Mattos' house. He couldn't be bothered to notice her existence between visits. He hadn't been consulted when it came to making holes in her walls, either. But you could bet he was looking forward to her funeral and to inheriting a nice piece of real estate in a town where property prices were going through the roof. "Tony was at summer camp," I repeated. "You mean when the bathroom was added? That summer?"

"Isn't that what I said?"

I smiled. "You're right. I wasn't paying attention. How old was he when he went to summer camp?"

"Only that one year, he went," she said. "Duarte was set against it. He said that's for the tourists an' all, that we didn't need no summer camp. The boy could work on the boat if he wasn't in school. But then that summer, he said it would be all right if I wanted Tony to go. An' I was happy enough to get him out of the house, seein' as it was a bad summer for my asthma."

"You don't have asthma," I pointed out.

"No one believes me, but I do," she said. "Those doctors over to the Outer Cape Health, what do they know?"

What, indeed. I smiled again. So Duarte Mattos, fisherman and penny-pincher, had all of a sudden enrolled his son in summer camp at the same time he moved his wife into a cousin's house and built a bathroom addition onto the house on Carver Street. I glanced over at Mrs. Mattos, at the stubborn angle of her chin. She had to have known. She *had* to have known.

I pulled into the parking lot at Stop & Shop, knowing from long experience that there wasn't going to be any conversation that didn't have to do with food, or the price thereof, until we were back in the car. But all the time we were inside, prowling the aisles and checking things off her list, my mind was going. There had to be some people around who remembered what was going on in the 1970s, and who would be willing to talk to me.

Napi's hadn't panned out, but I wasn't finished yet.

Once I got Mrs. Mattos home and her groceries unloaded, the Little Green Car safely in its parking space, I checked the time and headed back down to Commercial Street. It was late enough for the Old Colony Tap to be open, early enough for its regulars to still be coherent.

Walking in there is like walking into a piece of Provincetown's past. The Old Colony has a lengthy history of providing the fleet with its dosages of alcohol, and even today the stools are filled with the ghosts of long-ago crews, captains raising their glasses to safe trips home until the last one, the one that wasn't safe at all.

Mike had got me thinking about Norman Mailer, and if you think about Norman Mailer, you also have to think about Stanley Wolff, another legendary hard-drinking prolific writer who'd lived in the East End. Stanley was dead now—a stroke? a heart attack? I couldn't remember—but his son Hubert was an institution at the Old Colony. Living off his father's trust fund, Hubert could be found most days "working" on his boat, a once-beautiful sailboat that he spent most of the summer on. He had never, as far as I knew, actually done any real work for even one day in his life, and wasn't about to start now.

The Old Colony is, truth be told, a little scary. If you don't drink, you don't go there. It's dark and while it doesn't exactly smell of beer, it doesn't exactly not smell of it, either.

And Hubert Wolff was exactly where he'd been the last time I was in here. The barstool next to him was empty. I took a deep breath and went in.

***

"And then he told me he wasn't having none of that. Only he said, *any* of that. Had to be perfect, dear old dad. Use the language perfectly."

Well, I found myself thinking, since his perfect use of the language is what's enabled you to do pretty much nothing all your life, you might be a little more forgiving of the occasional curmudgeonly attitude. I didn't say it.

I had a feeling that Stanley Wolff wouldn't have even recognized his son. In his early sixties, Hubert could easily have passed for ten years older. He had a grizzled sort of face that hadn't seen a razor in a couple of days, blue eyes that squinted as though always looking into the sun—and this in the darkest bar in town—and clothing that could have used a good wash. Or maybe fumigation.

And he was on his third beer. I was still sipping my first. I'd gotten him past his deprived childhood as the son of a literary legend sent away to boarding school, and was easing him into summer memories of said childhood. "So you hung out with some of the other kids in town, didn't you? Maybe date some of the girls?"

He peered at me. "You looking to get raunchy?"

I could feel my cheeks flush. "Not at all," I said quickly. He looked vaguely disappointed and turned back to his beer. I kept talking. "I'm just trying to find out about someone—a girl who lived here then. She might have been around your age." Portuguese? Probably, in view of her resting-place, but not absolutely for sure. Better wait and see what Hubert came up with.

He finished his beer in one long swallow. "I wasn't the one of us who liked all the girls in town," he said, as though making an announcement.

I signaled the bartender. We were going to have to get somewhere soon, or Hubert wasn't going to be fit for anything but leering. "Who was it, Hubert? Who liked all the girls?"

He grabbed the new beer and took a long swallow. "Mr. Perfect," he said indistinctly.

"Sorry? Who was Mr. Perfect?" A thought occurred. "Your father?"

"If you ever met my mother, you wouldn't ask that question," he said.

So there was a trace of humor under all his sodden thoughts after all. I smiled. "Okay, then, who's Mr. Perfect?"

The guy on the other side of Hubert banged into him and I lost his attention for a minute or two while they loudly sorted it out. This, I decided, had been an exercise in futility. Whatever Hubert knew, he wasn't in any state to tell. I was no closer to finding out who was in that wall than I'd been, and I was rapidly becoming poorer, even at Old Colony Tap prices.

All right. I'd finish my beer and I'd leave Hubert to whomever he could next get a drink off. With his money, he should be buying for everyone in the room, anyway.

He swung back to face me just in time for a belch in my direction and I fought a sudden urge to get sick. Good thing Stanley Wolff had passed on to that great library in the sky, because he'd have killed Hubert if he could see what he'd become. And that Stanley was financing, on top of it all.

Not that Hubert looked like anyone's idea of a trust fund baby. They're supposed to at least dress the part, or that's what I surmised: my life hasn't brought me into contact with too many trust-fund recipients, which is probably just as well.

I gathered up my purse and said, "All right, it's been nice talking with you. I have to get going." I signaled "check" to the bartender and slid off my stool.

Hubert's arm shot out to stop me. "Don't you want to know?"

"Know what, Hubert?" I had a headache building and suddenly couldn't wait to be out of there, out and into the sunshine, away from the smell of beer and the sense of something that hadn't quite been attained. Maybe not even reached for.

"All about Gerald."

The bartender slid the tab over to me and I slid it back to him with a payment card. "Who's Gerald, Hubert?"

"I've been telling you. Mr. Wonderful. Mr. Perfect. Mr. Gets to Sleep With All The Girls."

Okay, maybe I was being a little hasty. I climbed back gingerly onto my stool. "Who's Gerald, Hubert?" I thought he could do with a little repetition.

"Had a girl here," he said, focusing blearily on my face. "Just the same as you asked about."

"Gerald had a girlfriend here? Who was she? Who was *he*?" How about asking too many questions at once, Riley?

To my amazement—and consternation—Hubert began to sing. "Maria!" he declaimed, his voice actually in the right range. "I just met a girl named Maria!"

"West Side Story," the guy next to him identified helpfully.

"West Side Story," Hubert agreed, and they clicked their bottles against each other's.

"Was her name Maria?" I asked. This was possibly too good to be true. Maybe he just felt like singing.

That must have been it. "I just kissed a girl named Maria!" Hubert wailed. The bartender was giving us funny looks. I grabbed Hubert's arm. "Did Gerald date Maria?" I asked. I still had no idea who Gerald was. Or Maria. But we were getting *somewhere*, anyway, weren't we?

Hubert focused on me again. "Mr. Perfect," he said, nodding owlishly. "Mr. Perfect. And Maria."

Breathe, Riley. Just breathe. I drew in a deep breath and held it for a moment, letting it out slowly. Good; now I felt less like shaking him. "When did this happen, Hubert? When were Gerald and Maria together?"

The guy next to him leaned over and said, "We don't talk about Gerald. Hubert gets upset."

"I get upset," Hubert agreed.

"Just tell me who he is, and I won't talk about him anymore," I said as persuasively as I could. I felt caught in an endless loop of Who's on First. "I'll go talk to him myself, you don't have to think about him again." It wasn't a name I recognized, not that I necessarily know everybody in town; the closest Gerald I could think of was Dr. Kinahan, a dentist over in Truro. Maybe Gerald was a recluse. Maybe he was someone everybody else called Gerry. The possibilities were endless. "Just tell me who he is."

Hubert was sadly examining his beer bottle, now empty. "Tell me about Gerald," I said again, slowly pulling my wallet out of my purse. I can offer bribes with the best of them.

He was watching, all right. "He went back to New York," he said, and actually licked his lips. "Dad said, no more fun in the sun for you. That's what he said. No more fun in the sun."

I stared at him. "Gerald's your *brother*?" I didn't know Stanley Wolff had any other children. Just Hubert, the failure, as Wolff had never hesitated to tell anyone who would listen. No wonder Hubert called Gerald "Mr. Perfect." But why hadn't I ever heard of him? Provincetown relishes the stories about its celebrities.

Hubert was nodding. "No more fun in the sun," he said again. "Never let him come back."

"Why?" I didn't really need to ask the question. I could see it already, unfolding in front of me like an old movie. I didn't know who Maria was, not yet, but when I found out I was sure I was also going to find the way she ended up in Mrs. Mattos' wall. And Gerald Wolff—it had to be—was sent away forever, probably because he'd slept with what his family deemed the help and, worse, gotten her pregnant. No more summers in P'town for him. No more fun in the sun.

Hubert was waiting. I slid a five-dollar bill out of my wallet and passed it to him; he waved it at the bartender. He licked his lips again. "Gerald," he said, "never came back."

No; I didn't think he had.

11

I met Ali and Mirela at the Mews restaurant in the East End a little after seven. She'd gotten the reservations; Mirela can get reservations anywhere, at any time. I don't know how she does it.

I kissed him on the lips and her on the cheeks and sat down. "Have you been here long?"

"Long enough to order cocktails," she said.

"That's long enough," I agreed and looked around for the waiter.

"I have been asking some questions for you," Mirela informed me.

"Oh, yes? About what?"

"About what, she asks," Mirela said to Ali, who grinned. "You should know by now, sunshine, that when you investigate, we all investigate with you," she added.

"Who said I'm investigating? I'm not a detective." That seemed to be becoming my new mantra. Bruce came over to the table, his eyebrows raised in interrogation. "Cabernet, please," I told him, and he went away again.

"Tell me you are not," Mirela said, accusing.

"You going to help me out here?" I asked Ali.

He shrugged. "Tell her you're not," he suggested.

"All right." I put my hands up in mock surrender. "As it happens…"

"I told you," said Mirela to Ali. He pulled out his wallet and passed a dollar bill across to her.

"Wait, you had a *bet* on this?"

"I thought you might resist," said Ali. "Clearly I was experiencing a moment of insanity."

Bruce came back with a tray of drinks. "Did you want a few minutes?"

"I don't," I said. I order the same thing every time I go to the Mews. I sometimes pretend to look at the menu, but even the specials don't tempt me. "Vietnamese shaking beef," I told him.

Ali ordered the vindaloo and Mirela the lamb loin chops, and Bruce gathered up the menus and went away again. I took a long swallow of wine. "You seem remarkably cheerful about this," I said to Ali.

He smiled. "I like skeletons," he said. "Their secrets aren't likely to come back and bite you."

"So you don't want me to tell you what I have found out?" demanded Mirela.

"Of course I want you to tell me what you found out," I said.

"So," she said, wiggling her behind into the chair as though settling in for a long-awaited chat, "Julie says this person, this woman, died perhaps in the 1970s. And I ask myself, what is happening in Provincetown in the 1970s?"

I sipped my wine, watching her. "And?"

"It was the golden age, sunshine," she said. "The golden age of Provincetown." She made it sound like all the words were capitalized.

I was skeptical. "It was hippies," I said. "Not—"

Mirela put up a hand. "Stop right there, sunshine," she said. "That is where you are wrong. It was a time of change. It was John Waters and Channing Wilroy and Philippe Marcade, and lots of drugs, and people behaving badly."

"And that's golden?"

She ignored me. "John Waters still comes here sometimes," she said. "And I know Channing, he lives off Pearl Street. I don't know what happened to Philippe Marcade, though." She took a swallow of her gin and tonic. "There was a girl named Black Beverly, and they say she took too much acid and walked backwards for a whole year because she had headaches, and walking backwards made the headaches better." She paused. "No one thought it was odd, this girl walking backwards everywhere."

Where did she *get* this stuff? "That's all fascinating," I said. But—"

"But nothing," she said impatiently. "I am coming to it. So many, many strange things were happening in town then."

"Right," muttered Ali. "As completely opposed to what happens in town now."

She didn't even spare him a glance. "And so some people who were famous were part of the crowd, and some people who were not, and some people who wished they were," she said, and broke off as the food arrived. We waited through the settling in, and for once I didn't immediately attack my shaking beef. Mirela pushed her lamb to one side. "And mostly they ignored the people who lived here," she said. "It is extraordinary. There were two hundred boats in the fishing fleet, and it was as if these people were living in an alternate reality, as if they walked down the same streets but they weren't the same streets for everybody."

I could just about sort that out. It wasn't all that different now, except that there weren't as many boats in the harbor. I started to eat my shaking beef.

"You are probably wondering where this story is going," said Mirela.

Ali was eating, ignoring us both. He popped a piece of naan in his mouth. "Go on," I said.

"Well, remember, sunshine, when I said to you that everything is about sex? And I was right. The people who came in from New York, they all were very laissez-faire about sex, yes? Straight, gay, bisexual, they all were doing drugs and having a good time and sleeping around."

The calm before the storm, I thought. The end of the innocence, before the plague hit in the 1980s and people started coming here to die.

She paused long enough to take a bite of potato and chew. "But always in the background are the other people, the townspeople, the Portuguese," she said. "And they did not mix so much with the city people, with these new people."

"They mixed with Norman Mailer," I pointed out. "Literally. Mixed it up. He used to get into fights with them."

"He went out looking for fights with them," said Mirela primly. "No one else wanted to. They were Catholic, they had work ethics, they were willing to take the money from these people but they did not want them in their own lives."

Ali said, "That's not so different from how it is now, is it?" He hadn't touched his glass of wine, though he was signaling Bruce for more water.

"Not so different," she conceded. "But it happened that there was someone who was pretending to be part of the crowd, the John Waters group, even though he really did not belong. He was from New York, too, but not an actor, not a musician like the others were." She sipped her cocktail. "He didn't understand the rules," she said. "All the others who came here, they kept their craziness to themselves, among themselves. The drugs, the parties, everything. Provincetown was a convenient backdrop. This was understood."

"Except...?" I prompted her.

"Except that this one person did not understand," she said. "He tried to be one of them, and he was not clever enough, or talented enough, to be anything but on the fringe. Perhaps that is why he broke the rules."

"You're making this last longer than you need to," Ali said. "Just come out with it. He got involved with a local girl, didn't he?"

"How did you know?"

He smiled. "Anyone could tell where this was going," he said. "Why don't you just get on with it?"

She shook her head, but said, "All right, so, yes, he got involved with a local girl. Perhaps involved is not the word; that implies a commitment of at least a few weeks. This was for fun only. It was never going to be anything else. At least, that is what I have heard. I don't know why *she* did it."

I thought about the quiet orderly households and a young woman peering out at the artists' antics from behind lace curtains. "I think I do," I said.

"So," said Mirela, "It did not end well. He thought he could do whatever he wanted, but they sent him back home, and he never did become one of the popular kids."

"And her?" I asked, picking up my wine-glass. "How did it end for her?"

"What do you think?" asked Mirela. "Un-less I am very *very* wrong, you are the only one who has met her. How do you think it ended for her?"

I put the glass down without drinking. "And the man?"

"He never had his father's talent," she said. "But then, who has?" The question was clearly rhetorical. She caught my eye. "Stanley Wolff's older son."

"Gerald," I said. Mr. Perfect.

She nodded. "Gerald."

Breathe, Riley: just breathe.

***

"It's all supposition, really," said Ali.

We'd worked our way through our meals and I'd ordered dessert and they'd ordered coffee. Ali still hadn't touched his wine. I'd caught his eye once and looked at it pointedly, and he didn't say anything, so I let it go. Something there I could figure out later. Right now I was all about sticky toffee pud-ding.

"But it is logical," said Mirela, eagerly. "And we could find out more, now that we have a direction."

I put down my spoon. "Who's this 'we,' white man?" I misquoted. "Are you a detective now, too?"

"I thought," said Mirela with dignity, "that you'd be glad of the help."

"You know," said Ali, sounding like a parent ignoring their kids' squabbling, "there are some other options."

"Such as?" I managed to not stick my tongue out at Mirela. Only just.

"Whitey Bulger was here in the seventies," said Ali.

"Have you been doing research, too?" I didn't know why I was feeling so annoyed. They were only trying to help. But it felt as though they were somehow stepping on my toes.

He glanced up. "Not for you," he said. "But when I transferred, of course I looked up Provincetown."

"Wait. You mean inside ICE. This has something to do with human trafficking?"

He nodded and stirred his coffee. At least he hadn't given up caffeine yet. "Bulger was into everything," he said. "Organized crime enterprises in Boston for decades. Drugs, weapons, girls. Lots of girls." He paused. "That body that was found in 1974," he said.

"The lady in the dunes," supplied Mirela.

"Right. That might have been a dumpsite for someone he killed in Boston. To make her an example."

"Not a great example, if no one knew who she was," I said.

"If he did it," said Ali, "then you can be sure the right people knew who she was. And I can't think she'd have been the only one. He spent time down here, stayed at the Crown and Anchor. Your girl might have been one of his girls, straight out of Ireland, came to Provincetown with him and got in trouble. In more ways than one."

"And ended up in the wall of some Portuguese fisherman?" I asked. "*Really?* That's stretching it."

"Probably," he said agreeably. "But you have to think about all the options."

He hadn't been thrilled about me considering all the options back when there might have been some danger to me; the fact that all this had taken place in such a distant past was enough to pique his interest. And I was still feeling irritated. In some strange way, I was feeling a connection to the girl in the wall. I was protective of her. Enough bad things had happened in her life; she didn't need people poking into all its nooks and crannies.

"If you're both finished," I said coldly, "I'm done for the night."

Mirela signaled for the check. "You do not have to be angry, sunshine," she said. "We are just trying to help."

"Maybe you shouldn't try so hard," I said petulantly. We were squabbling like children.

This is why we can't have anything nice here.

12

We were days away from the Portuguese Festival, and the streets were alive with anticipation. Chalk drawings of roosters were all along Commercial Street's pavement, while above it banners and Portuguese flags were fluttering gaily; there's always a breeze on the Cape. The big tent went up at Bas-Relief Park, and Mrs. Mattos invited me and Ali over for kale soup.

"Should I bring some wine?" I asked Ali. "Or—wait—maybe not for you? Maybe you don't drink anymore? Are you going to tell me what was going on at the Mews?"

He was writing in his red book. Agents keep logs of what they do, who they see, all that sort of thing; it's known as the red book. Until today I hadn't realized that it isn't, in point of fact, actually red. "You can bring wine," he said.

"But will you drink any?"

He sighed and closed the book. "I don't know."

There it was: that little frisson of fear. The feeling you get when you ask, "Are you seeing somebody else?" and expect the other person to heartily deny it, and then instead they pause before answering. This wasn't that bad, of course; but it felt like the first step away from me and into a new and scary Muslim identity.

Where I couldn't go.

I didn't say anything, just stood there, my hand on the kitchen cupboard, and after a moment he said, "I suppose you want to talk about it."

No. I don't. I don't want to talk about it. I don't want it to be *happening*, either. I don't want anything to come between us. I want everything to stay the same, forever and ever, amen. "I thought you were lapsed," I said. "The same way I'm Catholic."

"You mean by virtue of ancestry alone?"

I still had my hand on the cupboard. I closed it without taking anything out and hopped up to sit on the counter. This conversation clearly called for a little distance. "I used to go to Mass," I said, a little defensively.

"So ancestry and habit," he said easily. "Either way, it's not a commitment." He found his briefcase and put the red book in it. "But I'm not criticizing you," he added. "It's just—I'm trying to figure things out. What it means to be a Muslim."

"This is because of Karen," I said. "You know it is. She's made you think about it." Sydney Riley, master of the obvious.

"Maybe that's not such a bad thing," he said, and the claw of fear plucked at my stomach again. I was pretty sure that whatever flavor of Islam he was flirting with, there wasn't going to be space in it for me. There suddenly didn't seem to be enough air in the room.

"So you're going to stop drinking alcohol," I said. "I don't know, Ali, seems to me if you're going to embrace a religion it ought to be on a deeper level than just its rules."

"I didn't say I was going to stop drinking alcohol." He sounded irritated.

"Looked like it to me." I was pushing him, and I knew it, and I didn't want to, and I felt helpless to stop, as though I were being carried away on the tide of my own emotions.

My period wasn't close to being due, but the feeling was definitely pre-menstrual, that sense that drunken emotions are in the driver's seat.

He saw it, too. "This isn't a good time to talk about it."

"Oh? And when will be a good time? When you start praying five times a day? When you start wearing different clothes? When you—"

"I haven't started anything yet," he broke in, his voice mild.

"But you're going to."

He got up and crossed the room. He stood in front of me and eased my knees on either side of him and his arms around me. "This isn't about our relationship," he said. "I love you, silly girl."

"I'm not a silly girl." But I sounded pretty sullen all the same.

He reached up and kissed the tip of my nose. "You are if you think anything's going to change between us," he said.

I pushed him away and hopped down from the counter. "You can't say that," I said. "It's religion, Ali, for God's sake." *No pun intended.* "It's the most basic and important thing about anyone, and it changes everyone's lives. People go to war over it. People get killed over it." I stalked over to the sofa and flounced down on it, grabbing a pillow to hold against me. I had a feeling I was going to need the comfort.

"No one's getting killed here," he said, and he was sounding irritated again. "Sydney, I just need to figure out where I fit in."

"You're thirty-five years old," I snapped. "Isn't that something you're supposed to have figured out by now?"

"Maybe," he said. "But apparently I haven't."

"Apparently not!"

We were rescued from going any further down that path by the buzzing of my doorbell. We both managed not to make a crack about being saved by the bell, but I know we were both thinking it. I got up and opened the door.

It was Zack. "Hey, hi, Sydney," he said, and looked behind me. All the gay men look behind me when Ali's there. "Hey, hi, Ali."

"Hi, Zack," said Ali.

"What do you want?" I demanded.

"Just need your signature," he said easily, ignoring the tension he had to feel billowing out the door. He produced a clipboard. "Want to be elected for Fin Com," he reminded me.

Of course. The finance committee. Town government. Normal, everyday life. "Sure," I said, and signed.

"Excellent, Sydney, thanks." He glanced at Ali. "Sorry to bother you."

"No bother," said Ali easily, coming up behind me. "We were just going out anyway." He handed me my sweater. "We'll walk you out."

Which put paid to any further conversation we were going to have about religion, I thought. I was completely relieved, and angry at myself for being relieved. "Good thing we're going out," I muttered under my breath.

"What was that?" asked Zack.

"Nothing," I said. Sometimes I can be a complete idiot. *Just breathe, Riley, breathe.*

Mrs. Mattos' kale soup is legendary. In a town with a significant number of elderly Portuguese widows, each of whom has her own particular take on the famous Portuguese dish, and have had serious competitions to prove their talent, even in *that* town, Mrs. Mattos' soup stood out. Provincetown likes its kale with sausage—always linguica—or fish, red kidney beans, potatoes, and onions, slow-simmered in bacon or sausage fat, or braised in chicken broth until it's soft and sweet. And then everyone has her own secret ingredient that she adds to make hers perfect.

Mrs. Mattos' secret ingredient stayed secret; she'd give up her recipe, I figured, when she gave up her last breath on earth, and possibly not even then. But I'd had her soup before, and turning down this particular invitation wasn't even in the running.

Besides, I had some questions for her. And they had nothing to do with soup.

13

She made sure that Ali had three helpings. Of soup, of crusty bread, of salad. Me, she pretty much ignored.

Never mind; I wasn't just there to eat. "So, Mrs. Mattos," I said, once we'd complimented her several times on her soup, "who was Maria?"

Mrs. Mattos was in the act of passing the butter to Ali, and she froze. I've never actually seen anyone do that, though you read about it in novels. The accounts I'd read didn't really give a sense of the total immobility involved. Her heart probably stopped beating. A snapshot in time, I found myself thinking.

Then the moment passed and movement resumed, he took the butter dish from her, she wiped her hand on her napkin. "I don't know anyone named Maria," she said.

"But you did."

A shrug. "It's a popular name. Lots of girls named Maria."

"Let me see if I can help narrow it down," I said. "She lived here the year Tony went to summer camp, when you had the bathroom added to the house. She had a new boyfriend, too, and probably you didn't like him very much. I can't say that I blame you; I wouldn't have liked him very much, either."

Ali said, quietly, "Sydney."

I waved him off. "His name was Gerald Wolff," I said. "He was that fancy writer's son. And they sent him away because of what he did to Maria. He never came back to the Cape." I paused, and it was as though all three of us were holding our collective breaths. "What did he do to Maria, Mrs. Mattos?"

"She never lived here," she said, giving up.

"But she spent time here," I said. She had to have. I couldn't imagine that they'd brought her body here from somewhere else; she had to have died here. "What happened?"

"She went to the city," said Mrs. Mattos. "She went with that boy. She left us all behind for a life with him, and good riddance, we all said. Turn your back on your family like that."

"So she *was* family," Ali said, his voice gentle.

"My brother-in-law's girl," said Mrs. Mattos. I did a quick flip through her family tree, what I knew of it, but then gave up: it was too complex. "Summers come, and them people with it, and they act like it's their own personal playground, like none of us makes any difference."

Not all that much has changed, I thought. Second-home owners and tourists did the same thing now.

Ali said, "It was the writer's son?"

She nodded. "Eat the rest of that soup," she commanded him, the words automatic. "She didn't bring him round, that's for sure," she said. "She knew that no one were going to be pleased to see him, but we knew all the same. Always mooning about, she was. Acting like she's the first one ever fell in love." She snorted. "Like love was all that mattered."

"How old was she?" I asked.

She didn't have to stop and think about it. "Sixteen." It had already been on her mind.

I cast back to when I was sixteen. Maria had been right: at that age, love was indeed pretty much all that mattered. Poor Maria.

"He left and she left with him," she said, as though reciting something she'd learned by heart. "My Duarte, Manuel, her dad, everyone tried to get her back. But she had a taste of the city by then." She paused. "I never thought that boy had any honor," she said. "He was a foreigner and all, summer people, thought it best they should keep to themselves. But he took her with him to New York City, so maybe he did have some honor, after all."

"Except," I said, "that he didn't. Take her to New York City."

There was a long silence. "Who's Manuel?" Ali asked. He had obediently finished his soup.

"Manuel Silva," she said promptly. "Lives over to Nelson Avenue now, though back then was still in the neighborhood. Married that Lizzie Nickerson, but she's gone now, too," and she paused to bless herself, "with that cancer thing." She looked at us. "Manuel an' Maria, they would've been married, that was the plan, if she didn't run off with that writer's boy. It was all decided. Their parents had worked it out, and Manuel would be inheriting Joao's boat."

"Joao?" I was starting to feel a little lost.

"Joao. My brother-in-law. Duarte's brother," she said impatiently. Couldn't we follow anything? "Maria's dad, he was. An' don't think that he wasn't bothered by it, because he was, he jus' din' show it the way other people do. But he got sick after that, so as it ended up, Manuel got his boat anyways. And then he even added to that, got himself his own little fleet, nice little business, them Costa boys working for him now."

I cleared my throat. "Mrs. Mattos," I said carefully, "Maria was pregnant, wasn't she?"

She didn't meet my eyes. "Happens," she said briefly. "Din't need to be a whole business. Had been Manuel, wouldn't have been a problem, you see? They'd've got married over to St. Peter's a little early is all. Din't matter."

"But it wasn't Manuel. It was Gerald."

She sniffed. "My sister-in-law Sofia, she said, best thing Maria coulda done, running off, when all's said and done. Not what that Manuel wouldn't have done the right thing, come to it, he'd have married her anyways. Family's all that matters. We never thought that writer's boy would marry her, he were jus' summer people, but maybe he had more honor than we thought, as when he went, she went too."

"Only," I said again, "she didn't."

There was a long silence. "Let me help clear the dishes," Ali suggested, putting his

131

napkin on the table and starting to stand up. Her hand shot out and grabbed him. "Not senile yet," she said grimly. "I can clear my own table, thank you very much." But she didn't move, and after a moment Ali sat back down.

"It's Maria, isn't it?" I asked. "The skeleton in the wall?"

Her stricken face said it all.

***

I forgot that I was angry with Ali. "She really didn't know," I said.

We'd walked down to the Johnson Street beach together. The sky was streaked with the most garish colors imaginable, and I wasn't even admiring it. "She really thought Gerald had taken Maria back to New York with him."

"Well, if everyone said something had happened, why wouldn't you believe it?"

"*Someone* knew it hadn't happened," I said. "My money's on Mrs. Mattos' husband. Duarte Mattos. He's the one who suddenly decided to build an extension on the house and get her out of there. She'd probably been bugging him about an indoor bathroom for years. And he's the one sent the kid to summer camp, which they'd never done before and didn't do ever again. "

132

"It doesn't mean she was killed deliberately," said Ali. "There could have been an argument. She was his—niece, right? His brother's daughter? So maybe he was telling her to leave the Wolff kid and it got out of hand."

"How far out of hand does it have to be for someone to end up in a *wall?*"

He shrugged. We walked for a moment in silence, and I shivered, even though—for once—there was no wind. I slipped my hand into his. "Maybe she killed herself," I said. "And Duarte Mattos wanted to cover it up. The fishermen weren't always best friends with the police, even then."

"We don't even know how she died," said Ali. "Don't you realize that? It's one of the saddest parts of this whole sad story. It's all only conjecture until we know that, and I don't expect that's going to happen. Julie would have told you if it were anything obvious, anything that would have shown up on the bones." He thought for a moment. "Will there be a funeral?"

"I don't know." I didn't even know if Julie knew who it was. I should tell her, I thought. It wasn't a bunch of bones shoved into the most convenient spot to hide them; it was Maria Mattos, sixteen, pregnant and in love. She was becoming more and more real to me. "I wonder if Mrs. Mattos has any pictures of her," I said suddenly. "I didn't think to ask."

"Leave her alone for a while," Ali advised. "There's someone else who might know."

"Who? Duarte's dead, Joao's dead, Maria's dead."

"Think of Maria's generation," he said. "There's Tony, her cousin, who probably grew up with her, just a couple of years younger. And there's Manuel."

"Who thought he was going to marry her," I said. "I wonder how he felt about her seeing Gerald. I can guess it probably wasn't pretty. Townie girl with rich second-home owner, and a boyfriend in the wings. That's a disaster waiting to happen."

"More than just a boyfriend," Ali said. "Those two families were intertwined financially and culturally as well. He was set to inherit Joao's boat—*and* his fishing licenses, and they were probably worth their weight in gold. That's a lot to lose."

"That's right." I knew all about the fishing licenses; I was a little surprised that Ali did. The story of Provincetown is the story of the survival—or lack thereof—of small-scale fisheries, along with nothing less than the corporate takeover of the ocean, privatizing access to a public resource. The Portuguese had been struggling with it for years. The money didn't just go to the boat; the money went to the government. And then the government wondered why the fishermen resented them.

Everyone here knows the story. Back in 2010 a new system of federal fisheries regulation, called sector management, was started. In sector management a group of fishermen were assigned a quota to divide among themselves. All fine and good, except that in New England's seventeen sectors, an individual fisherman's share of the total allowable catch—his "catch share"—was determined by his past landings. That was grand for fishermen south of New England, where the daily quota on cod was up to two thousand pounds a day, but during the window of time used by fisheries regulators to determine catch history, Provincetown fishermen were allowed to land just thirty pounds of cod per day, so they got lower allocations under sector management. People struggled to make a living at something that had once been a financially safe way of life.

I cleared my throat. "Okay," I said, "where do we start?"

He smiled, not looking at me, looking across to MacMillan and the commercial boats tied up at the pier. "I thought this was your investigation," he said. "You pretty much told me and Mirela to keep our hands off."

"What, you're saying I can't have it both ways?"

He slipped his arm around my shoulder and hugged me to him, briefly. "Besides, much as I adore playing Watson to your Sherlock, I'm actually here for work," he said.

"Right," I said. "But the festival is about to start and you need to be talking to people in the Portuguese community who might have heard rumors about a shipment coming in. I'm offering you the opportunity to talk to fishermen. What more can you ask for?"

"When you put it that way," he said, and kissed me.

14

"The question," pronounced Mirela, "is, of course, who benefits?"

We were sitting at one of the bars at the Race Point Inn. I'd actually managed to pull myself away from my investigation long enough to do a little real work and prove that I did in point of fact have a job that didn't start with the title of detective. I'd called several couples and firmed up plans with them, spoken to my guys at the Cape Cod Symphony about some string quartets for upcoming ceremonies, and generally behaved like a real wedding organizer. I was feeling slightly smug.

Then Mirela dropped by and that was the end of that spurt of work. I was drinking orange juice; she was drinking some sort of energy concoction that she and Gino (this season's newest bartender) had come up with between them. He thinks they're going to market it and make a fortune. She thinks he's her personal drink-meister.

"Don't be ridiculous, you're not Hercule Poirot," I said. "Clearly Gerald Wolff benefitted. He didn't have to deal with a pregnant townie girlfriend."

"But it didn't *help* him," she pointed out. "Did it? Think about this! He never came back, did he? Hubert said no more fun in the sun for Gerald, and that is what happened. So it did not really matter at the end of the day, sunshine, what state his girlfriend was in." She paused. "At the end of the day, Stanley Wolff might have paid off the family, too, to keep quiet. Or perhaps they said it wasn't Gerald's baby."

I wouldn't have put anything past the Wolff family. But none of this was getting us any closer to what had happened to Maria. "I have to find Manuel Silva," I said.

"Good luck with that." She sipped her concoction thoughtfully.

"Why?" Finding someone named Silva in Provincetown wasn't a Herculean feat; figuring out which Silva one wanted was the issue. The family had deep roots in the community that sent tendrils out over time and geography. I couldn't imagine a street that didn't have a Silva in residence. It was just a matter of finding the right Silva. How tricky could that be?

"You think he is still a handsome young fisherman, this Manuel?"

She was mocking me, but I didn't care. "I think he's still a fisherman," I said. Manuel would be in his sixties—well, late sixties—around now; that's still working age. No one from the fishing community retires at sixty-five. No one can afford to.

Mirela made some sort of noise in her throat and sipped her drink again. "Remember when you first found the skeleton in the wall, and you thought it would be someone in the Mattos family, a—what did you call it?—a black sheep?" she asked.

"That was just a guess," I said guardedly. I had no idea where she was going with this.

"Well," she said, "there *is* a black sheep in this story, sunshine, but it is not in the Mattos family, it is a Silva."

"No." I put down my orange juice. "No. Really. Manuel?"

She didn't answer directly. "You know about the *Miranda Lady*," she said.

"No," I said again. "No!" The *Miranda Lady* was a famous—or infamous—Provincetown fishing boat. Sixty-six feet long and rigged as a trawler, it had been berthed at MacMillan for several years, becoming more and more derelict with every storm that went through. No one seemed to know who owned it, and no one seemed to know what could be done about it, except for someone who saw a commercial opportunity and started using it as either a nautical flophouse for homeless people or an informal needle exchange and drug site.

Rex the harbormaster got the town to finally look at the situation, and the *Miranda Lady*, barely seaworthy, was put out on one of the town's moorings, slowing the homeless and/or addicted traffic in and out of it from the pier at the very least. And no one really paid attention to it out in the harbor, even though it was pretty much the only thing moored out there in the winter; all the pleasure craft were in, and the working commercial boats all tied up at the pier. Alone out there, the *Miranda Lady* weathered the storms and didn't move. Ever. Until this past March when a nor'easter grabbed her as though she were nothing and flung her up on the break-water all the way in the west end of town.

"The *Miranda Lady* couldn't be Manuel's," I objected. "I heard the owner was that big fishing guy from New Bedford. You know, what was he called? The Codfather? The one who went to jail."

"Gossip," said Mirela, flicking the thought away with a flip of her wrist. I thought the dismissal was a little disingenuous, as she pretty much trafficked in gossip herself; but I didn't say anything. "No one wants to say anything about it, of course. But I have it on good authority that he is the owner."

I had no idea how she knew about *Miranda Lady* and the boat's purported ownership, but I didn't question it: Mirela doesn't get that kind of thing wrong. Instead I tried a different tack. "Is he living here? Or did he go to New Bedford?"

"What is your obsession with New Bedford?" she demanded crossly. "We were talking about Manuel Silva. And Manuel Silva owns the *Miranda Lady*, so everyone in town has something to say about him. And now there are three more eighty-foot trawlers, in addition to the one he inherited after Maria left."

"So," I said reasonably, "Where *is* Manuel Silva?"

"You won't find him anytime soon," she said. "He's out on Georges Bank, probably past it even, because he does not return until he has every fish he is allowed, and then a few more. He goes after the deep-water fish, the groundfish. They've been out for a month, and they won't be back until the Festival. It is bad luck to miss the Blessing of the Fleet."

"How do you *know* these things?"

She shrugged. "My friend Margaret looks after his dog when he's gone, as his wife has died, and she is starting to complain, he is gone more often than he is here." She paused. "And, sunshine, even if we find him, he is not the one to worry about. He was probably heartbroken when Maria disappeared. He would not have killed her. He did not benefit from her death. Someone else did."

"Unless it was an accident."

"People do not feel the need to put accident victims into walls." She finished her concoction and turned on the bar stool to face me. "So. We have Maria, pregnant and dead. We have Manuel, who was supposed to marry her and may well be out a boat and some lucrative fishing permits. We have Gerald, who probably got her pregnant. And then we have the rest of Provincetown." She sighed.

"You can count Gerald right out," I said. "He was sent back to New York."

"Ah, but when? What did he do, go to Stanley Wolff and say he's going to have to marry a townie? Right away? When did he find out she was pregnant? When did he leave?"

"I don't know." I could hear the frustration in my own voice. "Hubert's going to be no help, he probably doesn't even remember what year it happened, much less what month."

"We need more information," she said, stating the obvious.

I thought for a moment. "When you said Manuel was a black sheep, what were you talking about? Just that he owns the Miranda Lady?"

"Well, there is that. And perhaps black sheep wasn't the correct term." She paused. "My friend, Margaret?" she said. "It is Margaret Youville."

"So?" Of course she was; Margaret Youville is another accomplished visual artist in Provincetown, one of the few artists to continue the practice of white-line printing, which had originated here. The artists mostly know each other.

"So she lives next door to him."

I sipped my orange juice. "To the Wolff estate?"

"No, sunshine. To Manuel Silva, on Nelson Avenue." She took pity on me and for once didn't make me drag it out of her. "So Manuel Silva inherited the family house very *very* early, because his mother had cancer and she died when he was twenty and his father had already died, so there he was, with the house. And that was when Maria's father gave him the boat, so he'd have two, he'd be able to support himself."

"When did this happen in relation to Maria disappearing?"

"I don't know. We don't know exactly what year she disappeared, yet." There was that: Mrs. Mattos hadn't been forthcoming about details. It was pretty clear that she wanted the whole thing to just go away. "But what we do know, is it was the year the federal government started getting serious about limiting the quantities of each fish the fleet could catch."

"And Manuel overfished?"

"No," she said, and the light dancing in her eyes should have warned me. "He found alternative paths to wealth." She paused.

"Drugs?" I asked. It had to be.

She shook her head. "Guns," she said. "Guns from IRA sympathizers in Boston to the rebellion in Northern Ireland."

I sat back. The dates fit, all right. I vaguely remembered something I'd read, years ago, about a Gloucester trawler called the Valhalla seized off the coast of Kerry with tons and tons of weapons—guns, hand grenades, rockets, an amazing catch. That had happened sometime in the early 1980s, the article said. I'd paid attention because I was always interested in any history having to do with Ireland—my last name is, after all, Riley. And I'm nominally Catholic, but from what I knew about the Troubles in Northern Ireland, nominal would have been just fine; it was being Protestant that presented a problem.

"Gunrunning," I said. It would have been appealing, even to someone who didn't have a dog in the race, if I could mix my metaphors; Manuel would have been young, eager to make his mark, seduced by the money involved.

Mirela nodded. "Gunrunning," she confirmed.

"But people must have known!"

"Of course they did, sunshine," she said briskly. "And, what? You think that the fishing community is going to turn on one of their own? Rat him out?"

"No one says rat him out anymore."

"Maybe some of them were jealous, I don't know," she went on as if I hadn't spoken. "But no one would *turn him in.*" She emphasized the phrase for my benefit, even sketching quotation marks in the air with her fingers. "No one was going to do that. And with two boats, he probably employed some people, too. That should not be difficult to find out."

"So he *was* a black sheep."

"Well, gray, perhaps," she said judiciously.

"It doesn't get us any farther with Maria," I complained. "What?" She was staring at me as if waiting for something. "Well, what?"

"Sunshine," said Mirela, "what if he had started before? We keep thinking Maria was killed because she was pregnant. Perhaps that had nothing to do with it. Perhaps he had already made the connections. Perhaps she had found out. Perhaps she knew he was doing this thing—that was illegal and maybe even immoral." Mirela and I have a lot of discussions about what is and isn't moral. "Perhaps she told him to stop."

146

"But you said yourself that no one would have turned him in," I said. I felt like the floor was moving beneath us.

"There is a difference between not turning someone in and marrying them," she said.

***

Ali was unavailable.

I wasn't used to that. Generally when he's in P'town, he's here to see me, and he's taking a few days off from work to do it. I wasn't accustomed to him actually—well, *working*.

But since he was dealing with another kind of trafficking, he might—I thought—have some insights into the gun running of the 1970s and early eighties. Historically speaking, of course; neither of us had been out of diapers at the time. I'd just happened to read about it on Wikipedia.

Perhaps it was just as well, I thought as I sat at my desk behind Reception, absently chewing on a pen and listening to Edmund flirt with some guests. I really, really had to get some work done. It was Thursday, and tonight was when the festival officially started. The inn was full, the streets were decorated, and the mood was light. Maybe it would be good to think about that and not about something that had happened decades ago and had absolutely no bearing on the present.

Thursday of the Portuguese Festival typically kicks off with a fabulous dinner followed by dancing. The big white tent was up at the Bas-Relief Park, and tonight local chefs would outdo themselves producing and serving delectable Portuguese treats. Adrienne, the Race Point Inn's diva chef, had hired extra minions to do her bidding; and while she herself didn't go to the tent to supervise and serve her food—Adrienne never really left the kitchen, ever—she would know exactly what was most popular and what people were saying in comparing the food made by the various chefs in town. Adrienne is nothing if not competitive.

The tables were all ranged around the dance floor, and as soon as the restaurants packed up and left, the music would start in earnest. All the little kiosks that sold souvenir t-shirts and hats and books were staffed and already doing a brisk business, and I'd heard Edmund telling people that tomorrow's and Saturday's Dolphin Fleet whale watches were sold out.

The town was partying, and I should really get with the program.

I could just imagine, High seas, hard
rk, little sleep and bad weather: I didn't
y any of the fishermen their vocation.

She looked at me sharply, her little dark
s birdlike. "An' I never see you over to St.
er's, neither."

"I know," I said.

"It would be good for you to go, is all I'm
ing."

"I know." She was beginning to sound
e my mother. This was not a good thing.

She sighed. "Not for nothing, but it might
good for you. You could go to church.
u could start over with God."

"I don't know what I believe," I told her.
figure it's best not to visit someone's home
ou don't actually believe they exist."

"You might anyway. He believes *you* ex-
"

That was a fresh take on agnosticism, but
lidn't want to pursue it. Or Ali's conversa-
ons with Mrs. Mattos. "Did Maria go to
ass?"

She hadn't been expecting that. "It was a
ng time ago."

"But you know," I said.

"Of course she went to Mass. She was a
ood girl," she said firmly.

There was a pause. "Tell me about her."

There was already a line forming outside
the tent for dinner when I passed by on my
way home. I didn't generally do kickoff night;
more often than not someone scheduled a
wedding (thankfully, not this year) and anyway you really have to pace yourself to get
through the Portuguese Festival.

Mrs. Mattos was hovering in her doorway, lying in wait for me to arrive. "Well, you
took long enough," she said.

"Were we supposed to meet?" Was I losing my mind?

"Soup's on," she announced, and then I
understood. She wanted a taster. A pre-taster,
as it were. The big event of the festival might
for some people be the parade, or the Blessing of the Fleet, or all the Portuguese dancers;
but for Mrs. Mattos, it was all about the soup
tasting on Friday afternoon—tomorrow.
That was when the non-professional cooks
got to show off their family recipes. It was all
good-natured, of course, but bitter rivalries
seethed beneath the surface, and things happened at the soup tasting that were remembered and commented on all year long.

I smiled. "I was just hoping you'd made
some more of your kale soup," I said. Twice
in one week? Why not? "I should just go up
and see if my boyfriend—"

"Been and gone," she said, turning and starting to unlock her door. She had been standing in front of it and had still locked it. "Come on in."

I followed. What else was I supposed to do? "When was Ali here?"

"Had a talk with him," she said grimly. "No, don't be sitting there, over here." She dusted imaginary grime off the plastic seat of a kitchen chair and pointed me toward it. "Has a lot on his mind."

"I know," I said. A twinge of guilt was starting. Ali was trying to save lives. He was wrestling with questions of religion and identity. And all I could think of was to ask him to help me solve a mystery that was only really a mystery to me. Mrs. Mattos hadn't asked me to investigate; Julie hadn't asked me to investigate; I was doing this all on my own. Maybe my time could be better spent. What was that I'd said? *I am not a detective?*

Mrs. Mattos was watching me. "Okay," she said, as if reaching a decision, and turned back to the pot on the stove, lading the soup out carefully, placing the steaming bowl in front of me. The end of June isn't the best time for hot soup, and I could feel a trickle of sweat running down my back. Of course Mrs. Mattos didn't have air conditioning. She'd

grown up without it, ergo, could for it now. "Eat," she command

I took a first bite. Even on a soup was incredible. I wondere could ever get the recipe. Proba Mattos wouldn't trust her, a would never trust Mrs. Matto best," I said.

She nodded, her arms crosse bly under her breasts. "It is," Something else she and Adrienne mon: a complete conviction o worth. She turned to the sink, with cold water and set it down bowl, then sat down across the me. "He's worried," she said.

"Ali?" I frowned. "What did

"He worries about you," she pectedly. "He thinks maybe you happy with his religion."

He'd talked to *Mrs. Mattos* al had no idea what to say. "I have n to say," I said.

She traced the outline of her p mat with her finger. "My Duarte, much use in going to church,' "Funny thing, it's allus the wome to God here, but once them fishin; to Stellwagen, you can be sure t talking to Him plenty too."

She got up and bustled about, tasting the soup simmering on the stove, putting a dish in the sink. Finally, wiping her hands on a dishtowel, and just when I'd decided that she wasn't going to say anything, she turned to face me. "She sang," she said. "Fado. You know, Portuguese music. Like you hear to the festival, Saturday night. Music that's *saudade*."

I didn't want to interrupt, but she had paused. "What's *saudade*?"

"Means sadness. Longing." The word was uncomfortable on her tongue. "Fado is our music, Portuguese music, it's about the sea, it's about being poor. About sadness. And she sang it beautiful. Better'n any of them singers comes from New Beige or Boston. Better'n anyone come from Portugal, even. She had the sadness in her."

Another pause. I felt a stillness in the room. Not once since those bones were discovered had I actually truly thought of Maria as a person apart from her life and death and pregnancy. For me, she was a puzzle to solve, not a real, alive, vibrant teenager. And yet that was exactly who she'd been. She'd been in love. She'd sung fado. She'd had the sadness in her.

I cleared my throat. "She sounds… exceptional," I said.

Mrs. Mattos nodded vigorously. "That's true," she said. "Done good in school, too. Teachers all wanted her to go to college." She said it reverently, as if it were paradise, or Oz. "Her mother died when she was just young, an' her dad raised her. No other children. But he weren't around that much, was he, off to sea with them all the time. So she raised herself, really."

"I think maybe you helped," I said gently. The picture was becoming clearer now. No wonder she'd been here a lot, probably spending afternoons in this very room, sitting at this very table, looking at this same avocado refrigerator and stove; Mrs. Mattos' décor certainly hadn't changed since the 1970s. Father away at sea, mother dead; her aunt would have been the closest thing she'd had to a parental figure.

Well, Mrs. Mattos and God. But I wasn't ready to go *there* yet.

She suddenly brushed at her eyes. "She was a good girl," she pronounced again.

"When you heard she'd gone off to New York, it must have been painful for you," I said. "Did she say good-bye?" I'd just realized it was entirely possible that she really had planned to go to the city with the golden boy, and that maybe she'd come here to tell Mrs.

Mattos just that. Maybe I was underestimating Gerald Wolff. Maybe he'd defied his father and accepted exile from the summer house, but only if his own bit of summer came with him.

And someone else hadn't wanted her to.

15

I was feeling pretty chastised by my thoughts. My boyfriend was experiencing existential angst-related problems and I didn't want to hear about them, so he took them to someone else in town who would listen. I'd managed to uncover an old death—I couldn't even call it a murder, not until there was evidence of foul play—and I couldn't manage to scrape up a little compassion for the dead girl, only wanted the glory of "solving" the mystery.

Yeah, it was interesting, but academically interesting. Not interesting in a way that was going to change anybody's life. And in the

meantime I was acting like Provincetown re-
volved around me.

Yeah, Sydney Riley is amazing, all right.
Just not in a good way.

"Tell you what," I said to Mrs. Mattos,
my guilt kicking in overtime. "Can I take you
to the fado concert on Saturday night? I'd
love to hear it, and you can tell me about Maria." About Maria as a person, I added to myself: about Maria as she should be
remembered. Not as Miss Not-The-Detec-
tive wanted to remember her.

Mrs. Mattos was having none of it.
"What, I don't have no friends no more? You
think you have to take care of me? Every year
I go to the fado concert, and every year I go
with my sister Ana and her girls, and Beatriz
from over to Franklin Street, and now as I
think, I don't remember never seeing you
there, and now suddenly you want to take
me?"

I swallowed. "Okay, you make a point,
but—"

"But nothing," she said. "I'm doing what
I always do. You want to learn about fado,
good for you. You should. But you learn
about fado by being sad. By feeling the longing." She squinted up at me. "You ever feel
the longing?"

"How am I supposed to answer that?" What I was feeling was exasperated. Longing for something, sure, but probably not what she was talking about. "Fine, I just wanted to offer." And where the hell were Beatriz and Ana when it was time to take Mrs. Mattos to the Stop & Shop every week, anyway?

She made a gesture. "Go away, now. I have my soup."

Well, at least one of us knew what her priorities were.

Ali wasn't back until late, and I was trying to anesthetize myself with television when he got home. "Did you know," I said conversationally when he opened the door, "that *Law & Order* ran for twenty seasons?" I'd had to consult Wikipedia on my smartphone for that one.

He looked tired. "Actually, now that you mention it, I didn't," he said. He leaned over and kissed my forehead. "Hey, babe."

"You hungry?" Why did I feel like we were running through a script straight out of Middle America? *The Dick Van Dyke Show*, perhaps.

"No; I had something, thanks." He sat down beside me on the loveseat and Ibsen immediately jumped up into his lap. He stretched his neck and frowned at the TV. "You're *seriously* watching *Law & Order*?"

"It was that or *Star Trek*," I said lightly. "I didn't feel like thinking. It was that kind of night." I paused. "I went over and had more kale soup with Mrs. Mattos. She wanted me to be a tester. She's getting ready for tomorrow."

"Her soup going to win?"

"It's not an official competition," I said.

"It is, to her," he said and sighed, putting his feet up on the coffee table. "Coast Guard boarded a boat just inside the three-mile limit about two hours ago," he said. "One of the ones we've been tracking."

He wouldn't sound so tired if the news were good. I used the remote to put the television on mute. "And?"

"And if any cargo was there, it's gone now." He looked at the screen. "I like *Law & Order*," he said. "Everything gets tied up so neatly at the end."

Pity the real world couldn't be so accommodating. Neither of us said it.

"I don't know how much time you'll have in the next couple of days," I said tentatively, "and I get it that you might not have any, but if you want to do anything—have dinner, or go dancing, or watch the parade or something, that would be fun. You don't have to tell me now," I added quickly. "Just if you have time."

He smiled, and even when he was tired he was gorgeous. "Not sure I'm ever going to have energy for dancing again," he said. "But maybe dinner. Maybe the Blessing of the Fleet."

I nodded. "Okay."

We sat like that for a few minutes, with Sam Waterston talking silently to the jury in front of us. I didn't put the sound back on. I waited.

"I talked to Mirela today," Ali said, finally.

"Oh, yes?"

"She's spent time in Albania," he said. "I thought I remembered that she had. She did some kind of exchange program back in college. She's okay with helping out, if any of the leads pan out."

"She speaks Albanian?" I didn't know why I was bothering to ask; Mirela speaks everything.

"Reasonably well," said Ali, which meant totally fluently.

"Good, then." Another silence. I was going to have to do it. I took a deep breath and half-turned toward him. "Listen, Ali, I'm sorry I've been such a bitch about this whole—about you thinking about what it means to be a Muslim." Another deep breath. "Mrs. Mattos told me you'd been over there talking to her. And I thought—I feel terrible about that. That you didn't feel comfortable talking to me. Not that I made it easy for you. I kind of shut the door on it, and I shouldn't have, and I'm sorry."

He glanced at me, and then away. "It's all right."

When people say it's all right in that voice, it most definitely is anything but. "I don't know what else I can say." I sounded awkward, even to myself. And yeah, you do know what else you can say. "I think I'm scared of it. Because it's different from who I am, and I made all sorts of assumptions that you were more like me than you were different."

"I am," he said.

"I know, but you know what I mean," I went on. "It felt like something pulling you away from me. And maybe it is, maybe it will, but that's not up to me. You have to be good with yourself. You have to feel good about who you are and what you believe and how you live, and you won't if your girlfriend is having hysterics every time you want to talk about religion."

He took my hand, absently. "I don't know if I want to talk about religion," he said. "And honestly, Sydney? I don't know if this is about religion at all. I think it's about a be-lated sense of identity. Of culture more than any belief system." He shook his head. "I've never even read the whole Qur'an," he said.

"I haven't read the whole Bible," I pointed out. "Okay, yeah, I know it's not the same thing. And maybe I'm taking this too lightly, and that's not my intention. But— well, you know, a lot of people don't have the whole theology of the thing down. Whatever the thing is." I paused and swallowed. "That doesn't mean they shouldn't find out about it."

He slanted a look at me. "You mean that?"

I nodded and squeezed his hand. "Yeah, I do. I can't believe I'm saying this, you understand, but I do. It just took me a while to figure it out. Whatever it is that you're thinking, whatever got you started, whether it's Karen or your job or the world or whatever, you won't feel right until you've figured it out. And I guess—neither will I."

There was a silence. I think I'd maybe been waiting for some kind of outpouring of gratitude, like I'd just offered up my firstborn or something, but he just sat there looking at me, almost absent, like he was doing sums in his head. Okay, maybe this was worse than I'd thought. "I just don't know how I fit in, Ali," I said. "That's all. I know what you're thinking, you're thinking that's completely selfish of me, and of course it is, but that's the way things work. I want to be part of your life. And I'm not going to convert to Islam. And I don't know if you get really deep into it if that will be—oh, not good enough, that's not what I mean. But maybe *enough*, enough. That maybe you'll find you can't be with a lapsed Catholic anymore. That maybe things won't—work out, between us." Help me out here, I pleaded silently. I'm way out on the end of this branch all by myself and it's feeling really, really high off the ground, and really, really lonely up here.

"It's not just Karen," he said. Thank God; I was starting to think he'd lost his voice altogether. "Well, yes, it's Karen. I still think she's making a mistake. But it makes you wonder about commitment, and belief, and how to live the kind of life you feel good about living."

"I'd say rescuing Albanian women from slavery was living a pretty damned good life," I said, and immediately put up my hand. Somewhere in the past five minutes we'd let go of each other. I hoped that wasn't symbolic. "I know, I know, I'm doing it again. I'm not trying to take this lightly, I swear I'm not. And I get that it's different. What you do, what you believe, who you are."

"But it's not different," he said. "That's what I'm trying to figure out. How you live is as important as what you believe. And I've lived like someone who isn't a believer."

I managed not to point out that that was precisely what he was: someone who wasn't a believer. Until now, maybe.

"Maybe I'm not," he said, reading my mind. "But there's something… I don't know. Something beautiful about it. About believing in something bigger and more important than all the rest of this." He paused. "Something transcendent."

He had me there. But for one moment—one fleeting moment—I could swear that I smelled incense and heard Gregorian chant, saw the rich jewel tones of stained glass, felt the non-taste of a wafer on my tongue. For that one moment, I felt something transcendent, magic, untouchable. Something pure.

And then the moment was gone and I was back in my apartment, which is about as non-transcendent a place as you can imagine. And Ali was pushing Ibsen off his lap and standing up. "Just give it a little time," he said.

"All the time in the world," I said, far more calmly than I felt.

"Good, then."

"Good."

But it didn't feel good. It felt like a beautiful crème caramel that had a slice, just a sliver really, of glass hidden somewhere inside it.

***

I hate waking up, getting up, in fact just about everything about mornings. I'd taken half an Ambien Thursday night because I didn't want to toss and turn and make both of us crazy, but that always hits me the next morning. I was just at the point where my body seemed to be sinking down softly, gently, melding deliciously with the mattress, when the alarm went off. I grabbed my phone and hit snooze and groaned, feeling the sinking again. I wanted to stay here. I didn't want to get up and pick out what to wear and get dressed and make the bed and feed that cat and...

The alarm went off again.

Ali was already up, showered, breakfasted, and gone; he was spending the morning out at the Coast Guard station in the West End, doing whatever mysterious things law enforcement people do when they, as he calls it, "liaise." I'd very vaguely been aware of him moving about the apartment, but not so aware as to really surface out of sleep.

Now Ibsen was looking slightly indignant. I gave up and rolled out of bed. Friday, I reminded myself. Today is Friday. Things to do.

I turned the shower to cold at the very end and shivered while I was getting dressed, a nice change for late June. Ibsen got his breakfast, and I opened the refrigerator and there still wasn't anything inspiring inside. Some day they'll invent a self-replenishing refrigerator, and I'll mortgage my soul to buy it.

I texted Ali to see if he wanted to meet for lunch and got my bicycle out to head over to the inn. A curtain twitched across the street while I was strapping my purse into the basket and Mrs. Mattos peered out. I waved but she was already at the door. "It's Friday," she said.

"It is," I agreed.

"Will you be coming for soup?"

I nodded. "I just asked Ali if he wanted to come, too," I said.

She nodded vigorously. "He said he would, if he din't have to be somewhere else," she pronounced. She apparently knew more about my boyfriend's schedule than I did. "But you'll come, right?" There was a reminder of her age in the tone, a little uncertain, a little scared, and I smiled. "Of course I will," I said. "Try and keep me away!"

She nodded again. "That's good, then."

The inn was buzzing when I got there. That's what the Portuguese Festival seems to bring out: this sense of excitement, of something exotic happening. The truth is that while I love all Provincetown's theme weeks, many of them are really an experience for the group itself. We all enjoy seeing the bears come to town, but Bear Week activities are really just for bears—and rightfully so. Fantasia Fair is pretty much a spectator sport for anyone not directly connected with the Fair. The International Film Festival is wonderful for moviegoers, but doesn't really seize the interest of everyone in town.

The Portuguese Festival is different in that anyone can participate. You don't have to be Portuguese. You don't have to be anything. You can do as much or as little as you want: enjoy the parade, listen to the music, dance the night away, celebrate the Blessing of the Fleet, and throughout it all, you eat, eat, eat. Usually all season we flock to the Portuguese Bakery on Commercial Street; during the festival it seems that the whole town turns into a Portuguese bakery, and you can smell the malasadas—friend dough—all over town. I'd already stopped in twice during the week for custard tarts, and yes, I can get them all summer, but there's something different about eating them during the festival.

The inn was decorated with flags and roosters everywhere, and Adrienne had hit a home run with the promised Portuguese-inspired menu. Even Mike seemed oddly relaxed. He followed me back to my lair behind Reception. "Sydney! Isn't this a *day*?"

"It *is* beautiful," I agreed, stopping myself from looking around to see where his customary anxiety was hiding. "Did you go dancing last night?"

He grinned vividly, like a little boy proud of an accomplishment. "I did," he said. "I even met someone."

So *that* was it. "You did?" I repeated. "Oh, do tell all!" I'd by then located my chair and wheeled it back where it belonged.

That little-boy smile again. "His name is Geoff. He's just here for the summer, but he's thinking about relocating. He's a graphic artist so maybe he could go freelance."

I swiveled the chair to peer up at him. "Okay, but what's he *like*?"

"Dreamy dancer."

"You're a pretty dreamy dancer yourself," I said. I've seen Mike in action. "Go on."

He shrugged. "I don't know. He's nice. He's funny. He makes me laugh."

"There's a lot to be said for that," I conceded. "When are you seeing him again?"

He blushed. He actually blushed. "Lunch."

"Today? Under the tent?"

He rapped his knuckles on the Reception divider. "Okay. Enough of Mike's private life." But he'd been delighted to tell me. "Who's supposed to be here, anyway?"

I turned back to my desk. "I don't keep the schedule. Who do you think I am, the manager or somebody?"

He smiled. "See you later, Sydney."

After he left I settled in to work. After the soup under the tent I had to get back to the inn in good time for my afternoon wedding, one that had been on the books for two years, which is one super-long engagement if you ask me. And it had all the bells and whistles— in fact, they'd been disappointed that I hadn't been able to secure a horse-drawn carriage for them. It's Provincetown, I explained, and we settled on a decorated pedicab instead.

I started making calls; I've learned from experience that it never hurts to make sure that everyone's on the same page on the day of the wedding. Provincetown isn't the most traditionally upscale venue for weddings on the Cape—for that, you pretty much go to Chatham—and what I do isn't even close to

169

what wedding planners in big cities have to do, but when I started out, that sometimes meant I had to pinch-hit at the last moment when someone didn't show, or was late, or forgot. Yeah, *forgot*. *Really?*

So I sat and talked to the florist, the musicians, the photographer, the videographer, the hairdresser, and just about everybody in the world (or so it felt) but my mother.

Who, of course, called. "I haven't heard from you in over a week!"

"I've been busy, Ma. Besides, Ali's here."

She sniffed. After years of trying to set me up with the offspring of various and sundry friends, she'd greeted Ali's appearance on the scene with suspicion. To my mother, he was as foreign as a frankfurter. "It's not mutually exclusive," she said. "You can still call your mother."

"Only if I have something to say." Okay, that was uncalled for, but she sends me over the top pretty much instantly. You don't know; you haven't lived with her.

She decided to ignore me. "Katie O'Brien got engaged," she said. "You know, Stella and Mike's daughter? That's what you could do! You could come up here and plan her wedding!"

"Ma, I don't live in New Hampshire. I don't know anything about wedding planning in New Hampshire."

She sniffed again. Anyone who didn't know her might think she had a cold coming on. "At least it would get you up here," she said. "I know you're going to say it's the season, but your precious season takes up too much of your life. We don't see you from March until November!"

Patently untrue; and if I could make it even fewer visits, I would.

She plunged on. "The Thomases are selling their house. Edith said they've had enough of winters here. They're going to move to Florida, and I just don't understand that. Why would anybody move to Florida? Florida doesn't have mountains. And everybody there is *old*."

I have quite a few gay friends who are quite young and live very happily away from mountains, but I didn't think my mother was talking about either South Beach or the Keys.

"And your cousin Marti was here last week. She stayed four days. What a nice girl. She said she was sorry she'd missed you."

I'd just bet she was. My cousin Marti is the kind of person who, growing up, had always tattled on the other kids. She always had clean hands, no matter what game we'd been playing or places we'd explored, and even as an adult she was relentlessly well groomed. She probably missed me because that left her without anyone around to feel superior to. My mother never lets anyone feel superior to *her*.

"We were looking at some of your old yearbooks, and Marti said how funny it is, how fashion changes. You were wearing some very odd sweaters back then. I'd never noticed until she pointed them out."

"Wait, Ma, you have my *yearbooks*?"

"Well, of course I have your yearbooks. Don't be ridiculous. How else could I have shown them to your cousin Marti?"

"Why do you—" I stopped myself. Damn it, I know better, and I still do it. I took a deep breath and looked at the calendar on my desk. My calendar was full. I was a valid human being. "Ma, I'm sorry, I'm at work, I can't do this now."

She bristled. "Do what? We're having a conversation. Which we don't do often enough, God knows, so you might show a little more interest. Marti's called me twice since she left, I guess that one conversation is too much to ask of my own daughter. I don't understand why you always have to be so dramatic, Sydney."

And I don't understand how I haven't killed you and ended up in prison for the rest of my life. Though I might just get away with self-defense. "I have to go," I said, a little desperately. She was starting to pull me down her rabbit hole, and I knew for certain that was one place I didn't want to go. "Ma, say hi to Dad for me."

"Oh, fine. Say hi to Dad, but what about me? If you'd married Tommy Richmond you'd be living down the street from me, now you're as far away as you can get and that man won't even marry you."

I couldn't even begin to parse the number of things that were seriously wrong with what she'd just said. "Bye, Ma." I clicked away before she could splutter anymore, my stomach twisting as it did whenever I even thought about my mother, much less had contact with her. The phone rang again immediately, and I looked at the caller I, sighed, and swiped on. "Hey, Vernon."

Vernon Porter, also known as his alter ego Lady Di and my wedding officiant *du jour.* "Well, Miss Bossyboots," he said. "So you're ready for this afternoon?"

"You were on my list of people to call," I said. "I just got off the phone with my mother."

He wisely ignored the last remark. "Thought you might want to come over for dinner after the wedding," he said.

"Oh, sweetie, I'd love to," I said. "But I'm waiting to hear from Ali. We might—"

"Bring him along! The more, the merrier!" Vernon is a master of the cliché.

"It's Portuguese Festival," I pointed out. "If we do anything, we'll probably be under the tent."

"It's quiche," Vernon said, as though to sway me.

"Tempting, but I'll pass for now," I said. "Three o'clock, right? You'll be a little early?"

"You really are a Miss Bossyboots," he said. "Yes, yes, I'll be there."

"Thanks, Vernon. See you then."

Between the two strong personalities, I felt like I'd been on the flattened side of a steamroller. Miss *Bossyboots?*

Things would get better as the day progressed. They had to.

16

It was hot and crowded under the tent, which was par for the course. Ali arrived at the last minute, sweat beading on his forehead, and it was as if the argument—had it been an argument?—from the night before had never taken place. We made our way through the soup line, stopping every two minutes to talk with someone we knew.

"It's like going to the Stop & Shop in the offseason!" I exclaimed when we finally made it to one of the big round tables. A few people were already sitting there—I didn't know any of them, miracle of miracles—and nodded and smiled to us before resuming their own conversation.

"Where's Mrs. Mattos?" Ali asked, craning his neck around to look.

"She's here somewhere," I said, blowing on a spoonful of soup. "You and she are getting along like a house on fire," I added, hoping he would take it as it was meant: a peace offering.

"She's a nice lady," he said mildly. "It's a hot day for soup, though."

"We'll go someplace air-conditioned afterward," I said automatically. I'm used to Ali being on vacation when he's in Provincetown.

"Sorry. Have to head back to the Coast Guard station when we're done."

I sipped my water. "Any news?"

"Something else is definitely coming in," he said. "I don't know when, and I don't know exactly what it is, but the guy we arrested in Boston? He's saying it's this weekend for sure."

And it was Friday. I shivered. One thing I do know about Ali's work is that traffickers are armed. All the time. And not just with handguns, like the one he sometimes carries. "You'll be careful, right?"

He smiled. "I'm always careful." But he's not. I know that, and he knows that, and neither of us ever says it. "You have a wedding today?"

176

"This afternoon," I said, nodding. "Bells and whistles galore."

"Who's the officiant?" He knows people in town almost as well as I do.

"Vernon," I said. "He wanted us to come to dinner tonight. Quiche. And he called me Miss Bossyboots." Ali burst out laughing, loudly. "What? *What?*"

He was beside himself with mirth. "That's perfect," he managed to gasp after a moment. "You *are* a Miss Bossyboots, sometimes."

"Hmph." I tried the clam chowder. Excellent. Mrs. Mattos had better look to her laurels.

Ali was still smiling when we kissed and headed out.

***

The wedding was... well, a wedding, right? The two men getting married were perfect (well, they'd had two years to prepare for this day, they'd better have been perfect). Matching suits, ties, boutonnières, and a sense of humor I'd found lacking in our numerous interactions over those two years: they were both wearing red high-top Chuck Taylors with their suits.

The mothers both wept, the flower girl stole the show, the string quartet broke into a surprising rendition of the Bee Gee's "How Deep is Your Love," and Vernon hugged everyone present. The grooms took off via pedicabs, the guests trooping along behind in taxis (I'd arranged for a clambake on the beach by way of reception), and I breathed a sigh of relief and started cleaning up.

That was when Julie called.

"I thought you'd want to know," she said. "They sent the dental records around locally, and I've got a name."

I already knew what it was. I already knew who she was. Wait for it—

"Maria Mattos," she said.

I nodded, then remembered that she couldn't see me. "I see," I said, and swallowed hard. If I'd already known, why did it feel like I'd just taken a punch to the stomach?

"She's your neighbor's niece," Julie was saying.

I swallowed again. "So are you going to investigate?" I asked. "It's not an archaeological artifact."

"It's not a homicide yet, either," she said. "Until they find otherwise, it's undetermined. There's no evidence of homicide. There's no evidence of anything. Not yet."

"What, a pregnant sixteen-year-old just suddenly dies, and there's nothing suspicious about that?" I demanded. I was balancing my smartphone the way people used to hold telephone receivers, between their ear and their shoulder, while I gathered up champagne glasses, and I could feel it slipping. I put the glasses down just in time to grab the phone.

There was a silence. "How do you know how old she was?" asked Julie at last.

I bit my lip. Oops. "Mrs. Mattos figured it out," I said. "I was going to tell you, but—"

"When? When exactly were you going to tell me?"

"I've been busy," I said defensively. "And who knew, she could have been wrong." No; she wasn't going to buy that.

"And you wanted to do a little investigating on your own," Julie said.

"And I wanted to do a little investigating on my own," I admitted.

"And so? What have you concluded?" Her voice was cold.

"I'm sorry, Julie," I said in a rush. "I didn't mean to step on anybody's toes. Your toes, I mean. It just did feel like it was kind of academic. And yeah, I did try and think about who might have killed her."

"You didn't get very far, I assume."

"Not very," I agreed. "I talked to some people. To Napi. And to Hubert Wolff."

"Hubert Wolff?"

"Yeah, he's Stanley Wolff's—"

"I know who he is," she interrupted. "What did he tell you?"

"Probably not anything you don't already know," I said. I sat down at one of the wrought-iron tables on the patio, still strewn with champagne glasses and cocktail napkins. "He basically said that his older brother seduced Maria and their father found out and raised holy hell about it. And Gerald—the brother—got sent away and never came back to P'town. Mrs. Mattos said everybody thought Maria went with him."

"Well, of course they did. There was a note."

"What?" Maybe being a real detective pays off, I thought. "What note? Where?"

"She mailed it," Julie said, "to some relatives in town. It said she had eloped and that no one would hear from her again, yadda, yadda, yadda. Love to everyone and farewell. Typical runaway stuff."

"Did it sound like her?"

"How would I know if it sounded like her?" demanded Julie. "Her family seems to have thought so. No one said anything different."

180

"Her parents weren't around."

"Emilia's husband Duarte was," said Julie. "Emilia was. They accepted it as fact."

"And yet," I said, "strangely enough, it wasn't." I cleared my throat. "Julie, if it wasn't foul play, then how did she end up in a *wall?*"

"Well," she said judiciously, "there is that."

"Someone put her in a *wall,*" I said again. I'd glossed over the pure horror of it; now it was hitting me afresh. "What if she were alive when she went in?"

"Sydney, we've thought of that," she said, patiently. "And there's sure to be an investigation. Just not by me." I was used to that: as soon as homicide's involved, townie cops play second—or fifth—fiddle to the state police, who act as the investigating arm of the district attorney's office.

I was still imagining it. No; she couldn't have been alive. There was a three-week margin; that's all there was to work with. Three weeks, when Mrs. Mattos was staying across town and Tony was off at summer camp. For all I knew, it might have taken someone three weeks to actually die. "She couldn't have been alive," I said.

"Of course not," said Julie. I didn't know if she meant it or if she was just trying to be comforting. I chose to believe the former.

"But it's still foul play," I said.

"Where do you *get* these expressions?" she asked, and then sighed. "Okay, yes, it's illegal to place a dead body into a wall. You're right."

"So you're going after them for *mishandling a corpse*? That's all?"

"I am not going after anybody for anything," she said. "The state police don't share their game plans with me. I'm sure there's going to be an investigation. I'm also sure that it's not going to be the top priority for anyone. It's a cold case, Sydney. The kind that people take on when business is slow. I'm sorry, I know you're interested and of course Emilia deserves an answer, but I just don't have one."

"It's not your fault," I said, my mind racing. "You just... Hang on, where's the note?"

"What?"

"The running-away note. Where is it?"

"The state police have it," she said, sounding nonplussed.

"But where did you find it? Where did it come from? Who had it?"

She paused, as though deciding whether or not I could be trusted with the information. Apparently I passed her inner scrutiny, because at length she said, "Sofia Mattos."

"Well, of course it's a Mattos," I said, ex-asperated. "Who's Sofia?"

"Married to Arsenio," said Julie, "who, before you ask, is Emilia's brother-in-law. One of Duarte's two brothers. Other one is Joao, who was Maria's father. If I understand things correctly, after Maria's parents died, she spent most of her time either at Emilia's house or at Sofia's." No mention of the husbands; the house belonged to the women. The men were away at sea. Irrelevant, almost.

"Maria mailed it to *her*?" That must have gone over well with Mrs. Mattos—*my* Mrs. Mattos, that was. "I wonder why."

"Probably because that was nominally where she lived," said Julie. "On Court Street. I don't think she ever stayed with Duarte and Emilia. Tony was there."

"Tony was a problem?" Oh, please God, let's not have this turn into a story of abuse.

"Not that I know of," said Julie, cautiously. "But Arsenio and Sofia didn't have children. So they had space and time that Emilia and Duarte didn't."

A Catholic family with no children? That had to be a first. "Why—"

"Because they couldn't," Julie interrupted. "And I don't know any more than that, so don't ask me. In fact, I've told you everything I know." That would be the day, I thought darkly. "And that's all you need to know."

"Hold on," I said. "If someone forged that letter, it certainly points to—I don't know, intent? Is that the word? Doesn't that make it murder?"

A silence. She was probably counting to ten. I have that effect on people, sometimes. "Sydney. Listen. There are all sorts of possible scenarios here. We don't know when she went into the wall."

"Yes, we—"

"She might have written the letter and mailed it before whatever happened, happened," Julie went on. "She might have planned to elope. For all we know, she could have eloped, died in New York, been brought back here for—"

It was my turn to interrupt. "That's ridiculous!"

"Maybe," she said. "But more absurd things than that happen every day. You have to keep an open mind. And remember that you're not the detective on this case. I'm not even the detective on this case, and in case it's slipped your attention, I'm the only one in this conversation who is, actually, a detective. So let it go. Enjoy the festival."

"How can I if—"

"Good-bye, Sydney," she said.

"Julie, don't hang up on me! Don't—" There was a decisive click. I stared at my smartphone. "She hung up on me," I said out loud.

It seemed, somehow, a fitting end to the whole day.

17

"So it's official?" Ali asked the next morning. "It's definitely Maria Mattos?"

"So saith the prophet, otherwise known as Julie Agassi," I said. "Apparently they matched the records to some dentist in P'town who retired eons ago but kept everything in his basement. Who *does* that?"

"Apparently, a retired dentist in Provincetown," said Ali.

"Funny man." I made a face at him.

He drank some coffee. He was sitting on the loveseat, with the *Cape Cod Times* open on the coffee table. It looked like a normal Saturday morning. But he was wearing his gun holster, and that made me jumpy.

I didn't have a wedding. All I had was a dead-end mystery and a boyfriend who wasn't going to have a very good day, by the look of things. I cleared my throat. "So it's probably today? That your boat's coming in?" Hadn't Bob Dylan written a song about that? The hour when the ship comes in?

He turned a page as though nothing else mattered in the world. "Probably today," he conceded without looking up.

"You're—it's going to be all right, isn't it?"

He drank some more coffee. "I hope so."

"You *hope* so?" Wow, way to go with the upper ranges, Riley.

He finally looked at me. "Yeah. I hope so. I always hope so."

"But there's a chance it won't?" And suddenly there were tears pressing against my eyeballs. I blinked furiously at them. I'd spent most of Friday thinking about a dead girl, and now I was contemplating a dead boyfriend.

There was music drifting in through the open window. Down at Lopes Square, the Portuguese dance troupes had started to perform.

He regarded me seriously. "There's always a chance it won't," he said gently. "Sydney, I'm not a shopkeeper. What I do, there's always a chance something might go wrong.

My clients aren't wedding guests or tourists. My clients are very bad people. And we've had this conversation before."

"I know." And we had. Several times. I was starting to annoy my own self with my whining; he must have been ready to throw me out the window.

Pep talk time. Maybe I just needed to be held and told it would be all right, even if that were a lie. But he was the one going out there. He was the one risking his life. And what he needed this morning far outweighed anything I might need. But the holster was spooking me. I took a shaky breath. "So what do I say? Good luck? Come back alive?"

He was looking amused, which somehow made things even worse. "How about I love you?" he asked.

I relented. "I love you," I said.

"Good. I love you, too." He closed and folded the paper, drained his cup, and stood up. "The parade," he said suddenly.

"Yes, what about it?"

"I might see you there."

I raised my eyebrows. "What is this, something cloak-and-dagger? You might see me there? I should pretend I don't know you until you give me the password?"

"I might be looking for someone there. Or not." He shrugged. "But I'll look for you, anyway."

"As well you should," I said as lightly as I could manage.

He went into what passes in my apartment for a bedroom and came out wearing a jacket. It was a hot day in June. Maybe he didn't care. I wondered if it were only on TV that people tuck their guns into the back of their jeans. For that matter, wouldn't a gun tucked into your pants fall out when you ran, as those same TV characters seem to be prone to do? And what if—

"Bye, babe. See you later." A quick kiss.

"Bye," I echoed, but he was already out the door.

Saturday and Sunday of the Portuguese Festival are insanely, wonderfully crowded. It's a lighthearted crowd. People walk around town in gorgeous embroidered clothes and there's a lot of music and laughter.

I headed over to the inn, where the guests were all reflective of the town's mood. The same people who would normally be complaining about things—what am I saying, who would normally be complaining about everything—were smiling at each other and at us. A towel got misplaced by the pool and the guest shrugged it off good-naturedly Edmund was chatting with another front-desk clerk, Carl, and they were both actually laughing. I could live like this, I decided.

Mrs. Mattos called midmorning. "Is that you, Sydney?" she shouted.

I winced. "It's me, Mrs. Mattos." As you called me, and all.

"I don't need you to take me to no fado concert," she said. "I got friends to go with. But I think maybe the parade."

"You want to go to the parade?" It's not as idiotic question as it might seem. Not everybody goes; it's hot and the street's crowded. People stake out their places with beach chairs in the morning, and the few shady spots are coveted and fill up quickly. Then again, compared the Carnival, the Portuguese Festival parade is sedate.

"If you're going, might as well go along," she said, almost grudgingly. "When will you pick me up?"

Whoa. No way was the Little Green Car going to be able to circumnavigate these streets; nor was my eighty-something neighbor going to be able to go down the hill alone, much less stand in the sun for an hour. What I needed was one of those motorized carts from the Stop & Shop.

That was it! Inspired, I clicked away from Mrs. Mattos and called Bruce at P'town Pedicabs. Yes, he'd send someone to pick her up. Yes, he'd bring her to the Race Point Inn. Yes, he'd arrange for her to be picked up after the parade had passed. I promised riches beyond compare and arranged a pickup time.

Mrs. Mattos was not amused. "I'm not going in one of them things," she said when I called her back.

"If you want to go to the parade, then you are," I said firmly.

"You going with me?"

"Of course I am," I said. I'll see you at your house and the pedicab will pick us up and we'll go sit on the porch at the inn and watch the parade. You'll see, it'll be fun." How much trouble could we get into?

Why do I ask stupid questions like that?

***

She was upset, though it took a while to figure out why.

Mrs. Mattos looked grim when we picked her up and sat rigidly in the pedicab on our way to Commercial Street. She'd removed her usual apron but still wore a flowered dress of a cut that might just come back into fashion in the next decade or so; and somehow that

191

made her look perfect for the pedicab, a picture out of a bygone era. If you discounted the young Bulgarian guy in bike shorts who was driving, of course. I got a chuckle out of the the way she looked everywhere but at the muscled buttocks propelling us forward with such ease.

The pedicab deposited us at the inn, where I'd roped off two chairs on the railing overlooking Commercial Street. If Ali came, he could hold one of us on his lap, I thought. I really didn't think he'd come.

I got her ensconced in her chair, where she still sat up as though expecting something untoward to happen at any moment, her purse on her lap, her eyes forward. I went off to the restaurant—Adrienne was nowhere to be seen, but Angus cheerfully poured me a lemonade for Mrs. Mattos—and she took the glass gingerly, as though I'd offered her hemlock.

I sat down in the wicker chair beside her. "Great view from here," I said inanely. But it was: our feet were just even with the heads of the people milling about, the excitement building as one could start to hear, in the distance, the sound of one of the bands. We'd gotten there just in time.

Mrs. Mattos nodded. She sipped her lemonade. I smiled encouragingly. Finally she made up her mind to speak. "I didn't go watch them dancers this morning," she said.

"Okay." I didn't see exactly where this was going. Was I supposed to have offered to take her to see the performance at Lopes Square? I hadn't actually gone down myself, so it wasn't as if I'd left her behind.

"Used to go," she said. Then, extraordinarily, she reached somewhat clumsily past her purse and her lemonade to pull a handkerchief from her pocket and bring it up to her eyes. I hadn't seen the glint of tears there; maybe it was a preventative measure. "That detective called me," she said.

Of course. "Julie," I said, nodding. "She called me, too."

Mrs. Mattos looked at me. "All that time," she said. "All that time I'm thinking how ungrateful, she don't care about her own people no more, off to the big city and not a word to us here, and now turns out she spent all that time sittin' in my house."

I pushed away the immediate, vivid image of a skeleton sitting at the dining room table. "I'm sorry," I said, awkwardly and inadequately.

She sniffed. "So many times I cursed her name," she said.

"You didn't know. You weren't to know," I said. "There was no way you wouldn't believe what they told you, believe that letter that came."

"To Sofia!" So that still rankled, too.

"She didn't send it," I said, inspired. "That's how you know she didn't send it. If Maria had really written that letter, she would have left it for you." Instead, of course, Sofia got the letter and Mrs. Mattos got the body. I didn't think I should go there.

The band was getting closer, spectators more restless as they sensed the start of the parade. Kids ran shrieking across the street. I counted at least twelve small Portuguese flags being waved more energetically.

A hand landed on my shoulder.

I jumped; of course I jumped. I think I squeaked, too. Well, who wouldn't? Too much thought of death and skeletons and darkness.

"Ladies," said Ali, leaning down to kiss Mrs. Mattos' cheek, and then mine. "Looks like I'm just in time."

"Almost late," said Mrs. Mattos severely. She had flushed slightly when he kissed her. I loved it.

"Ah, but almost doesn't count," he said. He propped himself up on the railing and smiled at her.

"Is everything okay?" I asked.

He nodded. "Looks like it."

That was a relief. But he was still wearing his jacket, which meant he was still wearing his gun.

And then, suddenly it seemed, the parade was upon us. The costumes were dazzling, little girls with colorful streamers in their hair, embroidered vests and hats for the men, bright dresses and headscarves for the women. It took me a moment to make the connection to Karen, but I put it resolutely out of my mind. This was supposed to be fun. Brass bands and then the Provincetown Portuguese themselves, carrying the banners that they'd carry in the procession on Sunday, the names of fishing boats long gone, crews long lost.

Mrs. Mattos stood up, a little shakily, and I put a hand under her elbow. She shook me off and leaned both arms on the porch railing instead. The music seemed to swirl around us, and the colors seemed brighter than ever. An old-fashioned fire truck, all red paint and glittering brass, went by. Ali slipped an arm around my shoulders. "This is so cool," he said. "Why didn't we do this last year?"

"You were in California?"

"Maybe that was it." He grinned. Something good must have happened this morning, I reflected, for this kind of joie de vivre. I wasn't asking; I couldn't, anyway. The bands, and the dancers, and the spectators were all competing for aural attention.

"You know," Ali said, his mouth close to my ear, "I think—"

I never heard what he thought. He froze and when I looked at him he was staring across the street. "Oh, shit," I think he said next, and then suddenly he was in motion, vaulting over the porch railing and pushing his way through the marchers.

I'm not a porch-vaulter myself, and if I'd thought about what I was doing I wouldn't have done it, but it was automatic: I slipped under the railing and took off after him.

We were moving east on Commercial Street, against the flow of the parade, and the only way to make any progress was to run straight toward them, ducking around as necessary, since the sidewalks were jammed with spectators. I kept my eyes on the back of Ali's head and kept running. "Excuse me—sorry—sorry!—excuse me…"

I had no idea what I was doing. The costumes I was passing turned into a blur of bright colors. I was also getting seriously out of breath and made a quick mental note to consider working out. And still we ran. This was ridiculous. Ali knew what he was doing. Ali was trained. Ali had a gun.

I finally stopped. What on earth was I thinking? Did I really want to see him in action? Did I really want to see him get *killed*?

I kept walking, just because—well, because. Holding my side, which had developed a cramp. I was in front of the Schoolhouse when I head his voice yelling at someone and so, without giving it any thought, I headed back behind the building to where there's a small parking lot for the galleries and WOMR, the community radio station that owns the Schoolhouse building.

In the parking lot there was a man facedown on the gravel with Ali kneeling over him, putting handcuffs on. He took one look at me and started shouting again. "What the fuck are you doing here? Get down! Get *down*!"

I cowered behind the closest SUV. Ali wasn't finished. "What do you think you're doing? Do you want to get killed?" All the while, he was hauling the other guy to his feet, hands cuffed behind his back. "Christ, Sydney!"

I stood up slowly. "I'm sorry," I said inadequately. "I didn't mean—"

He pulled his smartphone out of his pocket and keyed in a number one-handed. "Yeah," he said into it, never taking his eyes off me or his other hand off the guy. "I've got him. Corner Howland and Commercial." He paused, listening. "Yeah, well, what else can I do?"

He clicked off and glowered at me. "What possessed you?"

"I don't know," I said honestly. "I didn't think."

"For sure you didn't think! You—"

The guy in handcuffs, who looked like (and probably was) a wealthy fisherman, said, "Don't let me interrupt anything between you two."

"Shut up," Ali and I said to him in unison.

"I could leave, if you want some privacy…"

Ali jerked back on the guy's arm and he stopped talking. Ali's expression made it clear that the two of us were, however, far from finished. I tried to think of something useful to say, but there wasn't anything. It had been incredibly stupid of me to follow him. No argument there.

"I'm going to go back to the inn," I said finally.

"Good idea." He looked grim. I hesitated, hoping he might say something else, but he didn't, and I walked back to Commercial Street, struggling to get through the crowds. The heat really hit me, I could feel the sweat trickling down my back, and it seemed that every obtuse tourist on the street planted themselves in front of me.

What on earth had possessed me? Did I think that I could do anything *useful*? Ali was anything but a damsel in distress. I'd left Mrs. Mattos alone and probably frightened and risked my life and...

Okay. *Breathe, Riley, breathe.* Enough of the Catholic-school guilt. I'd done something stupid, not the first time, not the last, time to move on.

When I got back to the inn, Glenn the owner was sitting with Mrs. Mattos. Glenn's a bear—literally, a member of the tribe of large hirsute gay men—but overall a friendly one. Right now he had one of her hands in his big ones and was talking to her earnestly; she wasn't looking at him.

He caught sight of me over her shoulder. "Sydney! We were worried about you."

"I know. I'm sorry." The parade had passed, groups of people were breaking up, wandering about aimlessly, heading for the bars. I touched Mrs. Mattos' shoulder. "I'm sorry to have run off like that."

"What happened?" She seemed suddenly very old and very frail. She'd been through a lot lately, maybe too much for someone her age. Maybe too much for anyone at any age.

"Ali saw someone he thought he knew," I said carefully, learning against the railing so I could face her. Glenn didn't look like budging from his seat. Probably thought I was going to shoot her as an encore. "I thought I'd go and see if I could help." That made absolutely no sense at all, and Glenn frowned.

Mrs. Mattos was willing to grasp at it, though, and let it go. "I want to go home," she said firmly.

"I'll call the pedicab," I said, and Glenn stood up. "No; I'll have a car come around," he said. I looked at him apprehensively. He was, after all, my boss, and he didn't sound very thrilled with me at the moment. He reached down and squeezed Mrs. Mattos' shoulder. "It will be quicker and more comfortable," he told her.

More comfortable, maybe. With the streets as they were, I wasn't so sure about quicker; but I wasn't about to contradict him. "You'll go with her, Sydney?"

"Of course," I said.

"Good." Another look, and then he was off, and I could hear him talking to Edmund at the front desk.

She glared up at me. "This is how you invite someone out?" she demanded.

I think my mouth was open. That little-lost-old-lady act had been just that: an act.

200

"Why, Mrs. Mattos. You sure had Glenn fooled," I said finally.

She broke into a smile. "He's treating me to dinner here next week," she said primly. "And his car is taking us to the fado concert tonight."

"You," I said slowly, "are a deceitful old woman and one hell of a con artist."

She looked past me. "I think that's the car now."

Of course it was.

18

We sat for a long time in silence Mrs. Mattos waved me off as she got into the car. It wasn't a limo, just Glenn's own Mercedes driven by one of his minions at the inn, but she was as regal (and fragile-looking) as the queen herself as Glenn helped her in. She roundly refused his offer for me to go with her. We both watched it pull slowly back onto the street, which had just been opened again to traffic a few minutes before.

"So," said Glenn.

"So," I echoed.

"What was that about?"

I shrugged. "Ali went after someone."

He stroked his beard. "Ali's in law enforcement?"

"You know he is," I said sharply. Glenn had been around when Ali and I met.

He nodded. "What I thought." He paused. "And you're not, right? In law enforcement?"

"Oh, for heaven's sake! It was stupid of me to go running after him. You don't have to tell me. He's already done that."

"Okay." He turned to go back into the inn.

"Wait," I said. "Okay? That's all?"

"Can I tell you anything he's not going to? Just watch out for Mrs. Mattos. She's a nice old lady."

I snorted, but a look at his face told me I'd pressed my luck about as far as it was going to go. "Okay," I said.

I felt at a loss. I didn't have any weddings until the following week, and every bit of planning that needed to be planned had already been planned. I didn't want to hang around the inn and I really didn't want to see Ali until he'd had a chance to cool down. The fado concert at town hall didn't start until seven-thirty.

I did what any sensible P'townie does. I picked up my car and headed for Herring Cove to park by the ocean.

A big SUV pulled into the parking space next to mine and the window whirred down. "I hate to be the one to tell you this," said Mike, "but it's not sunset yet."

I turned off my music and smiled ruefully. "Just getting away from things for a moment, " I said. "Taking a break," he said, nodding in agreement. "It can do wonders for your life."

"I'd settle for just my *day*," I said.

His smile was amiable. "Been looking for you, actually."

What fresh hell was this? When the boss says that, it's not usually to give you flowers. Or a raise. "Why don't you come sit in here, so we can talk?"

I obediently got out of the Little Green Car and opened the door on the passenger side of his monstermobile. "So what is this, come into my parlor, said the spider to the fly?"

He laughed. "Hardly. That plaque for Barry came in the mail today, and I'm not sure where it should go."

Not the swimming pool area, I thought with a shudder. It was in our swimming pool that only a year or so ago I'd come across the lifeless body of Barry—my boss, Glenn's husband, and the owner of the inn—floating facedown. An image that still weaves its gossamer way though the darkest tendrils of my dreams. "What does it say?" I asked, temporizing. "The plaque?"

He was watching the water. "A couple boats coming in," he observed. Any vessel entering Provincetown Harbor has to go through the Race (for which Race Point is named), the spot where the bay meets the ocean and kicks up some unexpected and serious currents. Crossing the Race isn't a picnic, though when you see the old maps of the Outer Cape that list all the shipwrecks from before the canal was built, you'd probably be delighted to be invited on that particular picnic.

I pulled out the binoculars I keep behind my seat and looked where he was pointing. It's a game with us, identifying the boats. The first one was way too easy: the *Richard and Arnold* is a bright red Eastern-rigged dragger, and there just aren't that many of them around. The silhouette gave it away: in an Eastern rig, the pilothouse is located—inconveniently—forward. They haven't made them for a long time; I think the R&A was built sometime in the twenties. It's an iconic boat: it leaves Provincetown for Nantucket during the season to fish for squid, and the island doesn't even charge a docking fee, the boat is so photogenic; all the tourists love it.

Nantucket had a fleet once upon a time, too...

"Give me the glasses," said Mike. "My turn." He watched for a few minutes. "*Helltown*," he reported. For a time between when the Pilgrims were here and the fishing began in earnest, Provincetown was called Helltown. Now there's a scalloper by that name.

We sat for a long time in silence after that. Vacations can take on all sorts of guises.

***

I was barely in the apartment when Mirela called me. "I have tickets," she announced.

"Congratulations, I'm happy for you," I said. "Tickets to what?"

"Fado, of course," she said. "A customer gave them to me. He bought two paintings today. You can be my date." She paused. "And I have already talked to Ali," she said calmly. "He will not be joining us. He is otherwise occupied."

I winced. "He's still mad at me, isn't he." It wasn't a question.

"Oh, sunshine, he is, he is! But he will stop eventually. And you cannot blame him at the end of the day."

"I don't suppose I can," I said. "All right, let's go to the concert. I could use some sad, mournful, melancholic music."

"Now you are just being silly," she pronounced. "Meet me for a drink at Tin Pan Alley at quarter to seven." That wasn't a question, either.

Feeling like a twig carried on a rapidly moving stream with no real agency in what was happening to me, I took a long shower, fed Ibsen and spent some Quality Cat Time with him, and duly showed up.

All I can say is this: Mrs. Mattos was right. There was something magical about the music. The instrumentalists were all men; the singer was a woman, wearing a long black dress with a black embroidered shawl, long red fringes shimmering in the stage lights, and even though I had absolutely no idea what she was talking about, I found myself tearing up. Longing was the right word for sure.

Mirela, of course, speaks Portuguese. I've given up on counting how many languages she speaks, actually. "That one," she whispered, "it said, your eyes are not yours, they are two Hail Marys on the rosary of bitterness that I pray each day."

"Cheerful," I whispered back. The rosary of bitterness? And sixteen-year-old Maria sang these songs? I didn't really have a clue how to access that kind of emotion; how had she?

Maybe you have to be born Portuguese.

Everyone leaving town hall seemed appropriately subdued. "I'll see you tomorrow," I said to Mirela, and she grabbed my arm. "No, you don't," she said fiercely. "It's samba time!"

"I've had a day of it," I pointed out. "I'm ready to go home."

"Well, sunshine, you will not," she pronounced. Her eyes were dancing with merriment. "Now we have some fun!"

The band had already set itself up on Ryder Street next to town hall, and the street was filled with people. Some were dancing, some were watching the dancers, some just listening. It was as though the emotions, released by the fado, were surging in exuberance to the rhythm. I gave in. "Okay, let's dance!"

She laughing in delight and we did.

About a half-hour in, I was taking a breather when someone tapped me on the shoulder. "This one's mine," said Ali.

I stared at him. "You're speaking to me," I said slowly.

"Only if you'll dance with me."

"Deal."

Mirela had disappeared, and I scented a plot. Never mind. I was feeling great. No talking during samba, of course, and that didn't matter. Ali's a great dancer and seems to adapt to any style. He was raised with Middle Eastern music but the first time he'd taken me out in Boston it had been strictly ballroom; and now it was samba.

"Let's get something to drink," he suggested, and we headed over to one of the food trucks specially permitted for the festival. I bought Sumol sodas and we found one of the benches in front of town hall that almost had enough space for us both to sit on it. I held the cold bottle against my forehead. "I'm sorry for what I did, before," I said.

"I know," he said. "You scared me. I didn't—I don't want that world touching you. I don't want you to be any part of it."

"I get that." I took a long drink. "Can you tell me who he was?"

A wide grin. "It'll be in the papers tomorrow," he said. "They were Albanians, all right."

"He didn't sound Albanian."

"He wasn't." He took a deep swallow from his soda. "Just living off them. Who knows what nationality he's playing with this week, but we've been after him for a while.

Didn't expect to see him here; that was a bonus."

"What was he doing at the parade?"

"You know a better place in town for an anonymous encounter?"

"Picking up his cash?" I asked. "Don't they all do bank transfers these days? Something more high-tech than a parade in a fishing village?"

"Exactly. Who would think?" He stretched his legs out as some of the bench's other occupants left. "That was the whole point of this operation—and the others like it, all up and down the New England coast. Innocent festivals, boats, parades."

"But it didn't work," I said, feeling oddly elated about the whole thing. "Hang on, Ali—what happened to the women? It was women, right?"

"Yeah. In the trade, Albanians are women. They buy men from Africa, women from Russia and Eastern Europe." He caught my look and shrugged. "It's reality, babe."

I shivered. "I know."

"They're all good," he said, and drank some more soda. I watched more people go by, gaudy in the bright colored lights, laughing and chattering. The samba music was still pretty loud. "They'll take them to Boston, process them there."

"And then what?"

"Back home," he said. "Whether they want to go or not. Some do, some don't. They thought they were coming for legit jobs here."

"So this could happen to them again."

"I hope not. I don't know. I don't know what desperation can do to a person." He glanced away. "I've never felt that way."

Neither had I. We sat and drank and thought about it for a moment, and someone jostled me as he sat down on my other side. "Well. It's the girl who wanted to know everything about Mr. Perfect."

The fumes alone from his breath could have lit a torch. "Hubert," I said.

"Don't remember your name."

"Sydney Riley," I said. I didn't offer to shake his hand. "This is Ali Hakim."

Hubert peered at him. "Got a cigarette?" he asked.

"Sorry. Don't smoke." Ali was looking a little bemused.

"How about you?" Hubert asked me. He was looking slightly more down-and-out than he had at the Old Colony, though thankfully both times I was seeing him in semi-darkness. "I don't smoke either," I said.

"Okay." He took it philosophically. "Find what you were looking for?"

I shook my head. "I'm not even sure what I was looking for," I said.

"Sure you are," he said, surprisingly. He was sounding a lot clearer than he had the other day; maybe the smell of alcohol was less from his breath and more from having permeated into his clothes. "You're looking for a girl who disappeared."

Ali had his legs stretched out and was watching people in the street, but I knew he was listening. I took a sip of Sumol, swallowed. "She didn't disappear," I said.

Hubert was looking at me more closely than I found comfortable. "That's what I heard," he said, his voice steady. He couldn't have had a drink all day. I was suddenly glad that I wasn't sitting with him alone somewhere, that I had Ali's comforting presence next to me, that I was sitting on a bench on a crowded nighttime street.

"I suppose everyone knows by now," I said. The discovery of the body in the wall had been in the *Provincetown Banner*, the local newspaper, for heaven's sake; if finding it hadn't coincided with the Portuguese Festival, it would have been the only thing everyone would be talking about. As it was, I was pretty sure that it was all the *Provincetown* Portuguese community was talking about.

212

"Some of us more than others," Hubert said, and I forgot all about being uneasy. "Wait. You know something?"

"I know Maria Mattos," he said.

"Knew her," I said automatically.

A spasm of something like pain flickered across his face. "Knew her," he said.

I looked at him more closely. He face looked green under the lights. "Hubert," I said, "it wasn't just Gerald, was it? You were in love with Maria, too."

I felt Ali stir slightly next to me. Hubert didn't move a muscle. "Everyone," he said simply, "was in love with Maria."

That was starting to be a theme. "Tell me about her," I urged him. Hubert nostalgic and not drunk was an opportunity I wasn't about to miss. I couldn't believe it was past ten on a Saturday night and he wasn't under the table—or under the bar—but I was sure as hell going to grab my chance now that I had it. My friend Pat says that if you sit on the benches in front of town hall, eventually everyone you know will either walk by or be sitting there with you. Hubert's fortuitous appearance lent credence to her words.

For a few moments I thought he wasn't going to answer. I didn't want to look at him too closely; it was a little awkward sitting right next to each other and trying to carry on a conversation. I waited. Maybe he'd dozed off.

"She had the blackest hair," Hubert suddenly said. "My father called it raven's-wing black, her hair. He said you could write about hair that color." Oh, no, I thought: surely Stanley Wolff hadn't been in love with Maria, too? Maybe he was just being poetic. Hopefully he was just being poetic. "But it was curly," Hubert added. "She had these gorgeous long dark curls cascading down her back."

He paused. I swallowed. "She sounds beautiful," I ventured.

I could feel rather than see him nodding beside me. "She was," he said fervently. "She was an angel."

"Gerald's angel, though."

Hubert snorted. "Gerald's angel," he agreed. "He didn't realize how many other people loved her, too."

Was this simply the admission of a long-lost love, or a clue? I elbowed Ali. "You can join in anytime you like," I muttered in his direction.

"You're doing just fine." He was still admiring the view.

I thought for a moment. "Were you in love with her, Hubert?" I asked finally.

He made a funny snuffling noise and then said, in a rush, "Of course I was. Everyone was. When she looked at you, you thought you could do anything for her, you'd be willing to do anything for her. Like your heart might burst right out of your chest from happiness. Like nothing mattered, nothing in the world, besides her." He drew in a quick breath. "Like everything you'd always known was true was suddenly false, because it was just her that was true. She was the only true thing in my life."

"And in Gerald's life?"

"Gerald didn't understand. He didn't appreciate her enough until it was too late."

Ali stirred on my other side. "What made it too late?" he asked. His voice was gentle, liquid almost, sliding in so smoothly that Hubert probably wasn't even aware that I hadn't asked the question.

"Everything," and there was an edge to what he was saying, something I couldn't quite identify, something a little desperate and a little sad and a little off-key. "Dad sent him back to the city. Dad wasn't having his precious Provincetown reputation sullied. If anyone was going to be a ladies' man, it was going to be him, not his son. He wanted Mailer's reputation and by God he was going to get it."

"He was a good novelist," I said mildly. "As good as Mailer." Well, maybe.

"It wasn't the *writing*," said Hubert. "He had the writing, for Christ's sake. It was the whole bigger-than-life thing. He thought Hemingway was a god. He wanted to do it all, fight in the Spanish civil war, hunt rhinos in the Congo, seduce actresses in Paris. But he didn't have it in him. He wasn't Hemingway, he wasn't Mailer. All he really knew how to do was write. Nothing else. Not even how to be a father."

I didn't want to stop him, so I wisely— for once—kept my mouth shut.

Hubert didn't need urging, anyway. "He used to come here with his family and hole up in that mansion and pretend he's king of Provincetown. He's not even Portuguese. I mean, this was when the Cabrals were the real king and queen of Provincetown. Dad was New York all the way, and he never forgave them for not accepting him as one of them. Not that he ever really tried. He was condescending, and everyone knew it."

I knew about the Cabrals. Well, some of them; the family name is ubiquitous in this town. But Jennifer Cabral is one of my friends, and I could hear her voice talking over some long-ago beer we'd shared at the Pig. Jennifer calls herself the product of a "the crash between a Scottish-German iceberg and a Portuguese volcano." Her mother landed in Provincetown in the late fifties to study painting with Hans Hofmann; her father Reginald was an art collector and the proprietor of the Atlantic House "back when the voices of Billie Holiday and Nina Simone filled the dark corners," Jennifer told me. She really should write a book. "My mother and father were like the king and queen of Provincetown once upon a brief time, and they reigned with dysfunctional splendor."

Not as dysfunctional, probably, as the novelist glaring out of his windows and imagining himself larger than life, drinking with the fishermen, getting thrown out of bars, wrestling a shark in the harbor with his bare hands. That image was pathetic in too many ways to count.

But splendid? I didn't think there was much that was splendid about Stanley Wolff. Apart, perhaps, from his prose.

Jennifer's father was a legend in the intersection between the Portuguese, the artistic, and the gay communities of P'town. So many of his customers over the years were struggling young artists who often paid their bar tabs by giving him samples of their work. Reggie, who donated so many evenings of Atlantic House proceeds to so many charities that he seemed lucky to have anything left over for himself, nevertheless always seemed to have enough to buy art or literary memorabilia. By the time some of his customers— like Mark Rothko, Robert Rauschenberg, Larry Rivers and Franz Kline—struggled their way through to success, Reggie had assembled the core of an important collection, one he supplemented with regular purchases of works by Provincetown artists (including some who hadn't run up bar bills they couldn't pay). He used his house for a fund-raising exhibition of his Tennessee Williams collection, and he was quite proud that he was buying Robert Mapplethorpe photographs long before anyone had heard of the artist. Reggie's collection ended up in his house—where Jennifer and her husband live now—though most of the works were either sold at auction by Jennifer's sister, or are still in her possession. Jennifer only was able to keep the house after a lengthy personal and painful struggle involving wills, irrevocable trusts and broken relationships.

Cabral wasn't the only one connecting food and art in P'town, of course; Sal Del Deo opened Sal's Place and later Ciro & Sal's to keep himself in art supplies, and artists knew they were places they could get a meal and a little respect. Napi Van Derek had an

19

"Okay," I said again. "Enough about your father and his infatuations. What exactly happened when he sent Gerald back to New York?"

Hubert didn't even have to think about it. "He sent for her," he said. "Gerald, I mean: Gerald sent for her. For Maria. Back in those days, it was all Western Union, you remember?"

"Give me a break, I wasn't born yet."

He moved his torso away slightly so her could peer at me. "Really?"

"Thanks for nothing, Hubert. Go on. It was Western Union. That's for telegrams, right?"

outstanding art collection before he opened Napi's and filled the restaurant with his finds.

Stanley Wolff, on the other hand, had let Provincetown know that as a town, it was definitely second-rate in his book. Like Reggie Cabral, he filled his mansion with great art, but paid top dollar for artists with more hype than talent, and none of them with local connections. He'd tried buying a bar back in the eighties, and ran it into the ground in one season with inflated prices (even for P'town) and patronizing service. So he'd huffed back to New York, where he'd written novels with poisonous little barbs at Provincetown, then showed up summers expecting to be treated like royalty.

Which brought my thoughts back, full-circle, to Hubert. I cleared my throat. "But your family kept coming back to P'town." I hesitated. "Was it sour grapes? Or was it—"

"Of course it was Maria," he said.

Of course it was Maria. I was starting to see this girl as an unhealthy nexus of men—uncles, fiancé, boyfriend, admirers, stalkers—all of whom could potentially wish her harm. The question was less who would kill Maria, and more who wouldn't.

I glanced at Ali, who nodded. "I'm going to go find Mirela," he said, standing up in one graceful fluid motion. I nodded.

"It was," said Hubert with a note of infinitesimal sadness in his voice, "always Maria."

I'd just opened my mouth to respond when one of two men passing by stopped in front of us. "Sydney!"

It was Mike. I love Mike. In fact, the truth is that I owe my life to Mike. But I'd have cheerfully blotted him out of existence right then. His timing was atrocious. Just as I was getting somewhere... "Hey, Mike."

He drew the other man closer. "Sydney, this is Geoff. I've told you about him. Geoff, honey, this is Sydney."

"And he's told me about you, too," said Geoff with a smile, leaning over to shake my hand. "Pleased to meet you." His hair looked orange in the colored lights; I assumed he was as handsome as Mike thought he was.

"And you," I echoed. I half-turned toward Hubert, but he'd edged himself away and was looking in the other direction. "Having a good festival?" I asked instead.

"Fabulous!" said Geoff with more enthusiasm than anyone should be able to muster this late at night. "I've never been to one before. It's fantastic!"

"Did you go to the concert?" Mike asked. I felt rather than saw Hubert shift beside me, and I didn't want to lose him. "I did," I said

quickly. "It's so great to me
hope to see you again."

"You will," said Mike, an
and slipped his arm around
hoped he was right. They we
gether. If I hadn't had issues o
on my mind, I'd have been ev
them both.

But I had other fish to fry.
morrow?" I suggested, and watcl
appear down Commercial Stre
back to Hubert. "All right," I
"Now we have to talk."

"And for wiring money," he said. "He sent the money and—"

"Where?"

He frowned. Someone swore and dropped their red plastic cup filled with beer in front of us, and he lost the plot for a moment. I had to pull him away from the smell, which was clearly both distracting and tempting. "Where did Gerald send the money, Hubert? Do you know? Who did he send it to?"

I finally got his attention back again. "Her father," he said. "He sent the money to her father. And he wrote to her there." His eyes weren't seeing Commercial Street anymore. "He wrote her a letter that said he loved her and he wanted her to come to New York. He hadn't had time to find her before Dad made him leave, you see. But he sent a ticket with it, a train ticket. He said he couldn't come back because of Dad, but he wanted her to come to New York. He told her he wanted to marry her."

"Marry her? Really?"

He nodded. "It was Maria," he said simply. "You didn't know her. You wouldn't understand. Anyone would have wanted to marry her. She laughed, she was always laughing. She could make you feel like there was something good in the world after all. When I think of her, I think of her laughing."

Did he spend a lot of time thinking about her? "Except when she was singing fado," I said.

"Yeah, maybe that was it. There was that sadness inside. Even when she was laughing. Like she knew something was going to go wrong, but she was going to enjoy life while she could."

A mere sixteen years of it, I thought. "Hang on," I said, as another thought occurred to me. "Hadn't her father died? Hadn't *both* her parents died?"

Hubert nodded. "Not her real father," he said. "He died when she was a kid." I managed not to point out that she'd never been anything but a kid. "Her uncle Arsenio, he was the one she thought of as her father. Over on Court Street."

I racked my brain but there were way too many Portuguese names swirling around in there. "The one who got the letter," I said.

"What letter?"

I stared at him. "She wrote a letter," I said, "saying that she'd gone to New York to be with your brother. Except that of course she didn't really write it. And she sent it to them." Sofia, I thought. Sofia, and…

"Arsenio," Hubert said. "Arsenio Mattos."

"We need to talk to him," I said.

224

***

Mrs. Mattos took care of that.

Ali was already home and watching a movie with Ibsen when I got back to the apartment. "Got a message for you," he reported. "Mrs. Mattos called." He clicked the remote to pause the movie. "Says she tried calling you, but I think your phone's probably still off from the concert."

I checked it. "Damn; you're right. What did she say?"

"We're invited to go out on one of the fishing boats for the Blessing tomorrow," he said. He consulted an envelope on which he'd scrawled notes. "She says it's you and me, and her brother-in-law and his wife."

"Sofia and Arsenio," I breathed. Timing is, in fact, everything in life.

Ali nodded. "She's organizing the whole thing. I gather it's an honor, to go out on one of the boats?"

"A thumping great honor," I said, nodding. "Whose boat is it? Arsenio's gotta be in his eighties, it can't be his boat."

"This is the part you're going to love," he said. "It's Manuel Silva's."

I sat down on my one decent chair, staring at him. "You're kidding."

"Nope. Apparently his fleet—do you call it a fleet, when it's four boats?—docked yesterday and offloaded, and they've been decorating them ever since."

"Everybody decorates the boats," I said automatically. "There's a contest, and a prize for the best."

"Okay," Ali said agreeably. "So we're supposed to be at Flyer's by noon. They'll take us out to the boat while the procession's happening from the church." He glanced at me. "And there's more."

"What?"

"The name of the boat," said Ali, "is the *Miss Maria*."

I was still staring at him in shock when my phone started playing Aerosmith. It was Mirela. I grimaced and swiped. "You'll never believe what Manuel Mattos' boat is called," I said by way of greeting.

"The *Miss Maria*," said Mirela. "I know. And she is up to anything."

"Up to something," I corrected automatically. "Who's up to something?"

"Mrs. Mattos." She was tired enough to sound impatient. "She arranged to go out on it for the Blessing."

"I know," I said. "She invited me and Ali. Well, that or commanded, I'm not sure which." The corners of Ali's mouth twitched.

I got up and went over to the refrigerator. Nope; still nothing new in there. "What about you? Are you going?"

"No, sunshine. I am in the procession."

"You are?" This was news. "Why? You're not Portuguese."

"Delicately put," said Ali.

"I have been invited," she said with dignity, "to help carry a flag."

Talk about honor. "Okay, congratulations," I said. "But it's late, Mirela, and—"

"This is not why I called you," she said impatiently. "At the end of the day it does not matter what I am doing tomorrow. What matters is what Mrs. Mattos is doing tomorrow."

"Which is?"

She took a deep breath. "The Fisherman's Mass is at 10:30," she said. "And the procession gathers itself and walks down to the pier after that. With the bishop leading it."

"Right," I said encouragingly, as she seemed to be pausing. I knew the schedule already; the bishop was guest of honor at the luncheon at Race Point Inn after the Blessing. I'd gone over the plan, the menu, the seating, the protocol, with Glenn, with Mike, with Martin, with so many people it made my head spin to think about it.

"Mrs. Mattos knows the bishop," said Mirela significantly. "She has arranged to speak to him before the mass."

I still wasn't getting something here. "Why? A special blessing? A little gossip?"

"More like a little confession," said Mirela. "She is going to tell him something. She says she has something that is very heavy, it is on her conscience. I do not know what she is talking about. She will not tell me what it is. But she says she must talk to him before the Blessing."

I was too exhausted to connect the dots. "What's the problem? If she's—"

"I don't know, sunshine," and I could hear the fear in her voice. "Something is very, very wrong. I do not think it is safe for her."

"Not safe?" I echoed, and Ali raised his eyebrows in interrogation. "We'll be with her tomorrow, Mirela. Ali's law enforcement. How much safer can she be?"

"I do not know! I know that this does not feel right, this conversation with the bishop. I think that she is going to push someone. Do not ask me who. I do not know."

I shook my head. "Mirela—"

"Never mind, then! Just be careful to-morrow. Be very careful tomorrow."

She clicked off and I looked at Ali. "The oracle has spoken," I said, "and I have no idea what she said."

***

I was reminded of an old vinyl record my mother used to play. For all I know, she still does, though humor seems to be something she's gradually grown out of over the years. The record was of a Canadian comedy duo called Wayne and Shuster, and one of their acts was a recasting of Shakespeare's Julius Caesar as *film noir*. Calpurnia was, of course, the "dame" in the story, and I'll always remember her Queens accent. "I said to him, I said to him, Julie, don't go, Julie, don't go, it's the Ideas of March, beware, already!"

Maybe this year the Ides of March had been slightly delayed.

I slept poorly—not that I ever sleep particularly well—and finally got up around five o'clock so that Ali, at least, could get a little rest. Ibsen was delighted until he realized he wasn't getting a midnight snack—he's really mastered that look of total amazement and disgust rolled into one—and went back to bed with Ali. Those two.

Something was going to happen today. I wished I could figure out what. It was all down to Mrs. Mattos, and I didn't like her plotting, and I didn't like that she was doing it all by herself. She'd clearly connected some dots that I hadn't, and the old mystery ploy, "You may wonder why I've called you all here this evening" backfired more often than it succeeded.

I plugged in the electric kettle and waited for the water to boil. What was she going to tell the bishop? And what was he going to do, once she'd told? Confession is sacrosanct; he wasn't going to be able to use anything that she said to him against anybody else, report it to the police, nothing. So what was the point? Just getting it off her conscience?

It had to be more than that, or she wouldn't have made sure we were all part of the group invited to Manuel's boat for the Blessing. I've known Mrs. Mattos since I moved into Zack's apartment eight years ago. She's never invited me to do anything during the festival. She might herself have gone out for the boat parade—her husband's old boat had been sold for scrap years ago, since son Tony wasn't interested in continuing the tradition, the idea of ten and 12-hour days out at sea in the cold apparently not appealing to him, and I couldn't say I didn't understand that—but if so, she'd never spoken to me about it. We'd only really gotten close over the past year or so, when she decided that she'd prefer to have me take her grocery shopping than manage the van from the Council on Aging. So anything might have happened before, and she'd never thought I should be included in whatever it was she did at the festival.

The kettle whistled and I poured boiling water over the coffee in the French press. Maybe she *wanted* people to know she was speaking to the bishop. Maybe that was the point. Why else would she have called Mirela, which pretty much guaranteed that the news would be all over town within fifteen minutes? Was she trying to force someone's hand? To do *what*? As far as I could tell, nobody had done anything illegal, in this century at least.

Old crimes are still crimes, but there didn't have to be quite this level of immediacy to the response. There was something else going on.

By the time the sky was getting lighter, I still hadn't figured out what it was. Ali and Ibsen were still asleep. I moved around as softly as I could—not that real stealth is possible in an apartment this size—putting on a sleeveless green dress, slipping into my flowered sneakers, combing my long hair and putting it back into a ponytail. It was early enough that the beach would be deserted, or almost so, and I could feel the urge to walk. Maybe that would help engage my brain. "Hope on, hope ever," I muttered under my breath as I let myself out the door.

The eastern sky was doing its morning pyrotechnics routine, streaking pink over Truro, lighting up the clouds, and the blue that came up around it was that soft springtime blue, a Mary Poppins blue. Nothing bad could happen, I thought, under a Mary Poppins sky. I went down through the Johnson Street parking lot to the beach and walked along the water. Low tide, and a lot of small boats pulled up on the sand, most of them of the kayak or dinghy persuasion. In the offseason, some of the fishing boats let the tide strand them; it's a cheap way of hauling out and doing work below the waterline, or a way of making a quick fix in the season. It looked like someone had decided to do just that, and I strolled down the beach to see out of little more than mild curiosity. It was a destination, that was all.

It wasn't a fishing boat, though; it was a dilapidated sailboat. And the person scraping barnacles off the bottom was Hubert Wolff.

Too late to turn around; he'd already caught sight of me. "You're up early," he observed.

For someone who could be reliably found most afternoons and evenings at the Old Colony, he was a pretty early bird himself. "Hey, Hubert."

He hoisted himself up the ladder and re-appeared on the very tilted deck, ducking into the cabin for a moment before re-emerging with a can of Miller Lite in his hand. I breathed a sigh of relief: at least the world hadn't turned completely upside down. He popped the top and drank down half of it in one swallow. "Come on up," he suggested. "Have somethin' to show you."

I squinted up at him. "I'm fine here, thanks."

"No, really." He gestured toward the rope ladder. "I won't bite. I won't even leer."

"How many of those have you had, Hubert?" It was barely seven-thirty.

"Not as many as I'm gonna have." He gestured again. "Come on up, Miss Detective. Have some things to tell you."

I went. If worse came to worse, I was willing to bet that I could outrun him.

The deck was cluttered; Hubert lived on the boat in the summertime, and it showed. I shoved a few empty beer cans aside with the edge of my sneaker and sat a little tentatively and a little precariously in the tilting cockpit. I imagined it must be like this when it was sailing fast, though it had probably been years since this boat had sailed anywhere, fast or not. Maybe this was what it felt like when a boat tipped before rolling over.

Pleasant thoughts.

Hubert disappeared below again and his hand appeared, a can in it. "Want one?"

"No, thanks," I said. "Never before eight, that's my rule."

"Good one." His head popped out again and he pulled himself up back into the sunlight. "Good rule."

"Works for me." If he had changed since last night it didn't show. Hell, if he'd *slept* since last night it didn't show.

He pulled the tab off the new beer and drank. I watched him warily. He reached into a pocket and pulled out his wallet, flipping it open, pulling a grubby piece of paper out of it. "Here you go," he said, leaning across, holding it out toward me.

It was a color photograph of a girl in a checked dress sitting in a swing. Her hair was tied back with a ribbon that matched the peach color of the dress, and she was laughing, Deep dimples, olive skin, dark shimmering hair that Stanley Wolff had described as raven's-wing black. Maria Mattos.

I looked up at Hubert. "What?" he bristled. "You think we didn't have cameras back in the seventies? It wasn't the dark ages, you know."

I had kind of been thinking that it was. Pictures hadn't occurred to me. Why didn't Mrs. Mattos have any? "You're right," I said, handing it back. "She was beautiful."

He nodded, tucking it back into his wallet. "She was," he agreed.

"You've been carrying that photo for a long time," I said. "What about Gerald? Does he still think about her, too?" If she'd had this kind of lasting effect on her boyfriend's younger brother, I thought, what had the boyfriend felt? Had he really been able to turn his back on Provincetown and Maria? Or had she meant more to Hubert than she had to Gerald?

"Gerald. Let me tell you about Gerald." He gestured with the can, nearly overbalancing, correcting with the careful attention of the inebriated. Gerald never had a life afterward. Nothing. Nada. Maria was the end of Gerald."

"What do you mean?" Had he, too, succumbed to alcohol? Was he living in some swank New York penthouse, living off his trust fund and drinking himself into oblivion every night? Or maybe he'd just given up after being sent home. Okay, fine, no townie girl, life goes on. Marriage to a debutante and two WASP children and a house in Connecticut with white pillars and a green lawn?

"Gerald," said Huber, leaning in and almost tipping again, "isn't Gerald anymore." He leaned back, pleased with himself. "He came back for her," he said suddenly.

I was startled. "Gerald came back for Maria? When?"

"When he found out that there wasn't anything else out there," he said. He wasn't slurring his words yet, and I wondered just how drunk he was. He was gesturing a lot with his beer cans, but he wasn't drinking all that much. "When he found out that at night the walls closed in on him. And food didn't taste like food anymore. And every girl he dated was a ghost. It didn't take long."

Maybe the timeline wasn't what mattered here. "What happened when he came back? What did your father do?"

"Dear old Dad?" He laughed, but there was no lightness in it, no humor. "Dear old Dad didn't take it too well. Dear old Dad wasn't used to people saying no to him. Didn't fit in with his view of himself as king of the world."

"So what happened?"

"He found out that she hadn't been quite as faithful to him as he'd been to her." His voice had hardened, and I shivered. It felt as if a cloud had passed over the sun, even though that clearly hadn't happened. Down at water's edge, a couple of very small kids were chasing each other, shrieking. "She'd slept with someone else."

I leaned forward. "Manuel Silva?"

He was looking out over the harbor. "Nope," he said, and switched his gaze back to my face. "Me."

I blew breath out through my mouth in a rush. "Jesus, Hubert."

He looked away again. "She missed Gerald," he said. "That's all that was about. She was only ever thinking about Gerald."

I looked at him with something like pity. "You thought that you could be more like him," I said. "Is that what it was?"

"So he came back for her," he said, ignoring me. He was looking out at the harbor. The sun was up and shimmering on the water, almost too bright now. That kind of shiny bright day that was going to end in rain. Or tears. "But she didn't know."

"So what happened?" I asked again. I felt I was there only to prod him, that he would have been talking to the gulls without me as audience.

"Dad. Dad happened." He grunted and picked up a piece of rope from the cockpit floor; who knew how long it had been there, or what purpose it had once served. He was just moving it around in his hands; his eyes were still on the harbor. "Dad couldn't have disobedience," he said, the word sounding odd from someone his age. It was a word from the nursery. "Dad couldn't have anyone or anything that he couldn't control."

It seemed to me that there'd been a lot in life that Stanley Wolff chafed at not being able to control; his son must have been the icing on the cake.

"Dad," said Hubert, "decided to punish both of us. That was it. No more Provincetown. People were talking about us, anyway, and that was stealing his thunder. If anyone got kicked out of bars, it was supposed to be him. If anyone got a girl pregnant, it was supposed to be him." His gaze flickered down to the rope in his hand. "That's why he couldn't stand having us in P'town," he said, as though he were talking about something utterly reasonable. "In the city, no one noticed us. There were other literary legends with poorly behaving offspring. Here, it was just him."

"And Norman Mailer," I couldn't help but add.

"Norman Mailer was his nemesis," Hubert agreed. "He wanted to be Norman Mailer. And he couldn't be, so instead he became a second-rate Stanley Wolff."

It would have been sad, in a way, if it hadn't done so much damage. "How did he punish you?" I asked.

"What?" He seemed to have drifted off somewhere else.

"You said your father punished you and Gerald," I said. "How? What did he do?"

"He put an end to it all," he said, nodding owlishly. "No more special treatment. No more rich-boy perks. No more fun in the sun." I lost him again for a few seconds, and then he was back. "Marched us right down to the pier and put us on the ferry," he said. "Not this high-speed one that's here now," he added quickly, as though anxious for me to get the whole picture in my mind. "First year the ferry came back, 1972. The steamers stopped sometime in the 1950s, everyone wanted to drive everywhere, it was the new American way. But dear old Dad got us on the ferry to Boston the same day Gerald came back."

"Wait," I said. "He didn't even get to see Maria again? Gerald, I mean?"

"She'd gone somewhere," Hubert said. "That was it. She disappeared." He paused. "Seemed scared of something."

Maybe, I thought, of her boyfriend's brother. I wasn't entirely convinced that Maria had intentionally sought relief in Hubert's

arms. It sounded a lot more likely that the un-
intended consequences of sibling rivalry had
resulted in seduction... or rape.

And so Stanley Wolff, literary giant with
issues, had made sure that his sons weren't
going to cause him any more trouble. I imagined them, the big ostentatious car driving
down Commercial Street, down MacMillan to
the brand-new ferry. Everyone else excited
about the trip to Boston, the novelty of sea
travel. The two sons, boys really, sullen and
angry. No one was going to upstage Stanley
Wolff, not ever, not even his own family.
Maybe especially not his own family.

"So you went to Boston," I said.

"I went to Boston," he agreed. He tore
his eyes away from the harbor and the pier
where this long-ago drama had played out.

"You went?" I said. "What about Gerald?"

"You don't understand," he said, his
voice suddenly, inexpressibly gentle. "I loved
her. I was weak and young and stupid and I
couldn't stand up to my father, or to her family, or to anyone. I tried to make it right and
even there I wasn't strong enough to do it. I
wasn't man enough. I wasn't ever man
enough. But that doesn't mean that she
wasn't the only thing in my life that mattered.
The only thing in my life that was good. That

I did right. And I would have managed, I think, if I'd had time. I'd have broken free of him. I'd have done the right thing. I even tried. That was the year he had his stroke, and as soon as he did, as soon as I was free, I came back. I came back to find out about the baby. I came back to make things right. It could have happened."

I was staring at him. "Sure it could," I said.

"Then you understand."

"I understand," I said, nodding. "You killed him. You killed him because you couldn't kill your father and because he'd maybe raped your girlfriend." I leaned forward.

"Exactly how did you kill Hubert, Gerald?"

20

"So you do understand," he said, nodding. "I had to kill him. You understand."

"Not totally, to tell the truth," I said. "How did it happen?"

He shrugged. "Back then, there weren't all these cameras everywhere," he said. "I knew it was my only chance, I was getting this one opportunity and that was going to be it. Once we were in Boston, it would be too late. Dad was having us met at the ferry. He didn't trust us. Can't imagine why." He shook his head. "And the more I thought about it—the more feasible it seemed, you know? I mean, not just feasible, but sensible. It just was clear it was the right thing to do. He might even have raped her. You figured that out, didn't you? And my name was mud in this town, ironically enough, but his wasn't. Two birds, one stone sort of thing."

"How did you do it?"

"Took him into the bar first and got him drunk," Gerald said. It was odd how quickly I'd made the transition to thinking of him that way. "Not hard to do. Then we went out on the lower deck. Only two decks on that ferry, not like these days." He shrugged. "It scared me, how easy it was, to tell you the truth. Banged his head against the wall and threw him over. I waited for them to come get me. Thought for sure somebody would have seen. But no one came."

"You were lucky." Well, what else could I say?

He nodded. "Yeah, it did seem that way. No one noticed that he wasn't on board. No one noticed that he didn't get out. I knew there would be hell to pay in New York, but it was worth it. It was seriously worth it." He paused. "I was right, of course. But not in the way I'd thought. Dad had a stroke two days later. They brought him to Mass General and then transferred him to Mount Sinai in New York. He lived a while longer, but he didn't speak again. And I didn't speak to him." Even after all these years, there was deep satisfaction in his voice. "He died not ever knowing."

"He must have known," I objected. "That's probably why he had the stroke."

"Yes," he agreed. "I've always hoped so."

Nasty, I thought. And to think I'd once found Hubert—Gerald—pathetic. "So when did you come back as Hubert?"

"As soon as Dad kicked the bucket," he said. "It meant I didn't get all the money at once, I had to wait ten years for the lawyers to conclude that my dear brother Gerald was presumably dead, but the money didn't matter. I didn't need it. I didn't wait. I just came back to find Maria."

"What," I asked, truly curious, "did you think had happened to her?"

"Didn't think. Didn't know. Her family thought she'd come to New York. Manuel thought so too, else he'd never have gotten married, and he got married pretty damned fast. No respect for Maria. But by then..." His voice trailed off and I nodded. "By then you'd started drinking."

"My second love," he agreed.

"Screwed you up."

He nodded. "She wouldn't have been impressed," he said.

"Fortunately, she's not around to know," I said. "Maybe that was the plan."

He looked at me. "You think I killed Maria?" he asked. Nothing in his voice but mild interest. "I don't see her family covering up for Stanley Wolff's kid."

"No matter which one it is," I said.

He shrugged and went on playing with the line.

"So what now?" I asked. "There's got to be a reason you told me all this. You've admitted to murdering your own brother in cold blood." It sounded a little over-dramatic but I didn't know that I could manage to say fratricide with a straight face. "You know we can't leave it here."

"I know." He shrugged again. "This had to be coming one day."

"No, it didn't," I said. "I don't get it. You didn't have to tell me this. No one's been on to you. Chances are that no one was going to be. All you had to do was stay in the OC. And now... I don't get it. You'll go to prison for sure." Where they don't drink, at least not at the rate you're accustomed to. "You know I can't just let it go."

He shook his head. "Nothing's been the same since you found Maria."

"Technically, I didn't—" But I stopped myself. Technically, I had.

"See? It doesn't matter now. It just doesn't matter anymore."

I took a deep breath, stood up and checked out the time. Still only eight o'clock, but Ali was probably up and wondering what had happened to me. "I'm going to call Julie Agassi," I said to Gerald.

He nodded. He didn't look as though he cared one way or the other. If anything, he seemed relieved. "That's fine," he said indifferently. "I'll go to the police department on my own." He gestured toward the sand. "There are kids here. No reason to arrest me in front of them." He glanced up at me. "Don't worry, Sydney," he said tiredly. "Where am I supposed to run to? This boat's all I have."

I hesitated. Why was I suddenly feeling sorry for him? He'd been living free and clear all these years. He hadn't killed Maria, but he'd killed his brother. On the other hand... who knew how different sitting for decades on a stool at the Old Colony was different from decades sitting in a prison cell?

And why was I in a position to be making a decision that he hadn't even asked me to make?

Gerald was right about one thing: the beach was filling up. The sun was already turning warm and the last day—the best day, for some—of the Portuguese Festival had arrived. Back in the days when this had been a whaling and then a fishing center, there used to be giant fishing boats to lead the way, all decorated and fine, and every year people with names like Mattos and Silva and Cabral sighed as the numbers of boats in the parade diminished while the number of banners representing defunct boats in the parade and procession increased. Jennifer Cabral once said to me, "I miss the sight of them on Blessing like I miss my own mom."

The Blessing was all that and more. The Blessing was a reminder of the last people to live here successfully all year long. It was a reminder that these people have fortitude in their blood, the fortitude to withstand the hard winters and the even harder summers; and they still put streamers in their hair. When they all passed under the holy aspergillum it was an annual reminder that they were blessed to live here still.

At every Blessing of the Fleet, a vessel from the commercial fishing fleet is selected for the honor of leading the procession of boats in the ceremony, and the fishermen themselves choose which it will be; that boat's image is also printed on the back of that year's festival t-shirts. Honoring a fishing vessel is really about honoring the people who rely on that vessel to sustain families and communities. The Blessing of the Fleet is a tradition of hope—hope for a bountiful harvest, for good fortune, good health, and mostly the hope that the fishermen will always find their way home.

The decorated statue of St. Peter that's been carried down in procession from the church is put in that boat; and then the (and, truth be told, everyone that can fit) goes onto the *Provincetown II* slow ferry for the blessing. Mike Glasfeld, the owner of Bay State Cruises, recently added a small removable balcony for the bishop to use—sort of à la Pope Francis—and when he's done Rex gives a short speech talking about the tradition of the fishing fleet, the area, shares a story or two, talks about understanding what living in a fishing village actually entails... and then tells everyone to clear off so people can board the ferry and go home.

I don't know anyone who misses the Blessing. There are one or two boats that don't participate out of superstition—maybe once they went to the Blessing and subsequently had a bad catch, or went through a bad storm—but by and large, everyone's there. The commercial fleet goes first, with the big draggers—which are less maneuverable—first; everyone lines up outside the breakwater and then comes in.

Every time a mooring is rented or comes up for renewal, the harbormaster reminds boaters of the rules: let the commercial boats have pride of place; remember this is a solemn religious occasion; respect the bishop. "One year, somebody flashed him," Rex told me once. "Had to spell everything out after that!"

And this year's Blessing? Suddenly something in my stomach dipped. Something was going to go wrong, terribly wrong, I didn't know what it was, but I just knew it was, and I didn't know how to stop it.

One thing was sure. I wasn't going to change anything by sitting here talking with Gerald Wolff. He'd committed his crime decades ago. A few hours, now, wasn't going to make any difference. And I knew the police department had its hands full; the town had grown in size by at least a third for the Festival. "Okay," I said. "If you haven't gone to the police tomorrow, I'm talking to Julie Agassi."

He nodded. His eyes weren't even close to being on the same planet as I was.

Awkwardly I lowered myself down the rope ladder. Something made me look up at him once I hit the sand, and I still don't know why I asked him what I did. "You'll be all right, won't you?"

He waved me away tiredly. "I'll be fine."

Why should I care? Why *did* I care? I scrambled up the beach onto the softer sand above the high-water mark, my sneakers sinking in deeper, making it harder to walk. Gerald was no better off and no worse off now than he'd been yesterday, or last week, or last year. Sharing his secret with somebody hadn't changed his past or his present, only his future, and it was clear that he didn't care.

Whoever had killed Maria hadn't just taken one life. They might not know it, but they'd taken Hubert and Gerald along with her. That was an awful lot of murders, and I still didn't know who was guilty.

What I did know was that Mrs. Mattos probably had a very good idea, and I didn't see a way in which this was going to end well.

***

Ali called just as I was knocking sand out of my sneakers at the Johnson Street parking lot. "Where are you?"

"Heading back," I said. "Couldn't sleep." It felt like a really, really long time since I'd left the apartment.

"Okay," he said. "Do you want to just meet me at Flyer's? I can bring you a sweater if you need it." Ali knows about being out on boats.

"Okay," I agreed. Flyer's boatyard—founded by the late Flyer Santos, who lived to 100—was a good way down Commercial Street toward the West End, and the street was being closed off, readied for the procession. Normally if I were going alone I'd take my bicycle, but walking was good, too.

By now, I thought, Mrs. Mattos had spoken to the bishop. Nothing had exploded. I took that as good news.

I was still feeling a little haunted, and I wasn't even sure by what. Maria? Gerald? Hubert? The weird little love triangle that really wasn't a love triangle at all?

And Manuel Silva. It occurred to me, as I walked and ducked by revelers dressed in their finest and tourists dressed in their worst, that I was finally going to meet one of the players from the center of this drama. The fiancé. The fiancé who'd had the pretty girl promised to him and then taken away. The fiancé who'd built a small fishing empire, first on that girl's inheritance and then on—as absurd as it sounded now, half a century later—on gunrunning to Ireland. I wondered how it was that he'd never gone to jail.

I wondered about a lot of things. *Breathe, Riley.* Finally I pulled out my smartphone and called up Ali's contact number. "Hey," he said, sounding confused. "Everything okay?"

"Not so much," I said. "Are you on your way?"

"In ten minutes," he said. "I've been tying up some loose ends. What's wrong?"

I was feeling a little breathless, and it wasn't just from walking and talking at once. "Ali, Gerald Wolff killed his brother."

There was a pause. Ali isn't one of those people whose first reaction is, gratuitously, "What did you say?" He thought for a moment before responding. "Hubert is Gerald," he said finally.

"Got it in one." I dodged a family spread out across Commercial Street and meandering like a flotilla under heavy winds. "I think Hubert raped Maria when Daddy sent Gerald home. Gerald came back and got on the ferry and pushed Hubert over the side." I wasn't wasting words or breath here.

"And Maria?"

"She was already gone when he got back," I said. "I don't think they stayed around long after that."

Another pause. "Did you call the police?"

"No," I said. "I figured, it's kept this long, it'll keep until after the Blessing."

I'd known that wouldn't go over well, and it didn't. Law enforcement is a fraternity. "Sydney, you can't—"

"What? Where's he going, after all these years? It's a *footnote*, Ali. Julie'll take care of it later. He isn't going anywhere, he knew what he was doing when he told me. He told me *on purpose*." And I was still trying to work out why. "She'll deal with it, the state police will deal with it, the DA will deal with it. Tomorrow." I stepped off the sidewalk to accommodate two large bears walking in the opposite direction. "What's really bothering me is what Mrs. Mattos is up to. Did she talk to you?"

"No. Seriously, Sydney…"

"Oh, for God's sake, don't *seriously Sydney* me." The lack of sleep was catching up to me and he was getting on my nerves. "You want to arrest him? Be my guest. He's on his boat on the beach near Johnson Street. I'm on my way to Flyer's."

"Yeah, okay." He didn't sound exactly cheerful and well rested himself. "I'll be there as soon as I can."

"Okay. Bye." I clicked off. It wasn't exactly heartwarming, but I didn't have time for heartwarming. I didn't have time to think about Gerald. All I could now do was try and

253

make it all the way down Commercial Street, and keep my sanity in the process.

And wonder what the hell Mrs. Mattos was up to.

***

Flyer's was buzzing. The Blessing was meant originally for the fishing fleet—hence its name—but as the fleet shrank, the participation of other watercraft expanded, and now everything from yachts to day-sailors participated, and almost all of them decorated for the occasion. Not with the garlands of flowers and the saints' statues that the Portuguese boats had, but with a whole heck of a lot of other stuff. And Flyer's, as the marina of choice for a lot of the pleasure craft, was crowded as hell.

I made my way down to one of the floating docks and stood there looking lost until one of the kids that works Flyer's in the summer came up to me. "You the lady going out to Manny's boat?"

I glanced around. "Yes, but I'm waiting for someone else—"

"I'm supposed to take you straight out," he said. "I can't wait around. I'll bring them out when they get here. Coming after Mass, right?"

"Well, Mrs. Mattos is—"

"Emilia Mattos?"

What, everyone in town got to call her by her first name except for me? "Yes," I said. I didn't know if it were good news or bad.

There was a flurry of noise from up at the kiosk and someone came running down the dock. My fellow suddenly had all the time in the world. "What's going on?"

Tall guy, red hair, freckles. I can still close my eyes and see him. See his mouth opening. In my worst nightmares, the mouth opens slowly, the words come out decelerated, like an old 45 being played at 33 rpm. Low and slow and scary.

At the time, of course, it all happened very quickly. "Up to the East End," he was saying. "Guy ran his boat up on the beach and hanged himself off the bow."

I closed my eyes, the sun burning red against my eyelids. I could still see Gerald playing with that line, pulling it taut, testing its strength. It had been right in front of me and I'd done nothing. He'd asked me for time, and because it suited me, because it was what I wanted, I didn't pull out my phone and call the police. I didn't do anything.

"Is he dead?" someone asked. I didn't open my eyes.

"Yeah, that's what they're saying. Suicide."

I swallowed hard against the bile rising in my throat. Dead. Even Ali had said I should have done something. How didn't I see it? Why didn't I see it? Oh, God, I thought. He's dead and I didn't do anything but feel superior and condescending.

Someone poked me. "Hey. Hey! You okay?"

I opened my eyes and the wharf came back into focus, too bright, too busy. "What?"

"I said, you okay? You still wanna go out to Manny's boat?"

I looked at him blankly. "Um. Yeah. Yeah, I guess so."

"Then we'd better get going." He went ahead of me down one of the floating temporary wharves where a motorboat was tied up. "Can you believe that?" he said over his shoulder. "Some guy killing himself at the Blessing!" He held up a hand to steady me as I got on and sat down. "Never heard of that happening before," he said.

Yeah, I thought. Pretty memorable. And chances were, we hadn't seen anything yet.

The outboard roared into life and we backed neatly out, maneuvering deftly among the boats on their moorings, the Flyer's rentals, the summer yachts that people lived on while they were in P'town, and I barely saw any of them. I saw Gerald back when I thought of him as Hubert. Sitting in front of the bar at the Old Colony. Talking people into buying him drinks when he could have bought the building five times over. Talking about Maria as if she were a goddess. Looking exhausted and defeated down on the beach at Johnson Street.

And then imagining. Imagining him dangling from that line, over the sand, the kids around to see, to have nightmares for the rest of their lives. He'd even said that, he knew they were there, he'd said he didn't want to get arrested in front of them. "Fuck you," I said, out loud, and the slipstream caught my words and hurled them out over the harbor. "Fuck you, Gerald." Even dying he had to screw things up, even his death was selfish and cruel.

Everything I knew about Maria (and at the end of the day, as Mirela would have expressed it, I knew very little) pointed to the same thing. That she'd wanted something simple and yet her life, who she was, had set off a chain of events that popped like firecrackers and injured everyone in their wake.

I hadn't really been paying attention, but when I looked up, we were approaching the fleet. We'd just passed the Donna Marie—a scallop boat that supplies Cape Tip Seafood—sixty feet long, blue and white, and decked out like a beautiful bride despite her age. And then, right ahead of us, was the *Miss Maria.*

Something cold clawed at my stomach.

The kid yelled something up to the boat and a man came out of the wheelhouse, and waved. The kid reversed the engine and they threw a rope ladder over the side. I almost was sick at the sight of it, but suddenly it seemed everyone was yelling at me and I stood up and bounced around a bit before I could grab the ladder. I was only halfway up when strong hands took hold of my arms and hauled me up the rest of the way and I ended up on the deck. It smelled, not surprisingly, of fish. I felt like a bit of a fish myself, plopped down and definitely without my sea legs yet.

I didn't watch the tender roar off. I looked around and didn't see anyone I knew and started strenuously wishing that I were someplace more pleasant where I'd feel better. At the dentist's, say, and having a root canal. Maybe in front of a firing squad.

Manuel Silva was looking at me a lot more frankly than I found comfortable. He was very big and very strong and had so many tattoos on his arms that it was difficult to know where to look. Curly black hair going gray. Dark appraising eyes. "You the neighbor?" he asked.

Yes, well, we all know each other in contexts, don't we? "That's me," I said, sounding a hell of a lot more chipper than I felt. "Sydney Riley." I didn't put my hand out to shake his. For one thing, there was a little too much pitch. For another, his hand looked like it would crush mine completely.

He nodded, as though confirming something. "Come on in," he said, and I immediately starting coming up with reasons I couldn't go down below until I realized he was indicating the wheelhouse. Inside it was a little stuffy, but there were a couple of plastic-upholstered chairs bolted to the floor, and an elderly looking couple sitting in them.

They didn't look especially excited about seeing me. "We'll go out on deck for the parade," the woman said. "I'm Mrs. Mattos."

Of course you are. Just what I need. Another Mrs. Mattos. "Pleased to meet you," I said. So this was Sofia, who had raised Maria and had received the letter saying she was safe and sound. And had apparently never questioned it. "Mr. Mattos," I added, smiling at the man. He nodded back. Obviously chatter didn't run in this branch of the family.

The engines had been running all this time—I know enough about boats to know that you don't turn diesel engines on and off and on and off—but they assumed a higher pitch and I realized we were gliding through the water in the direction of the piers. "Wait!" I said, urgently, moving to where Manuel was standing at the wheel. "Wait! We're supposed to pick up someone else!"

He nodded, keeping his eyes on the harbor traffic. "Emilia," he said.

"No! Ali! My—friend." Somehow a thirty-something woman saying "boyfriend" sounded a little silly in this setting. I had no idea why. "We have to wait for him!"

Manuel shrugged. "Have to go pick her up to Cabral's Wharf," he said, as though I hadn't said anything.

"No!" My entreaties were making a big impression on him, I could tell. I steadied myself—definitely didn't have those sea legs yet, or anything even approximating them—and looked grimly ahead. Cabral's Wharf isn't actually that; it's been a while since the Cabrals sold it and it reverted to its original name of Fisherman's Wharf, but I wasn't in a position to correct Manuel. Hell, I wasn't in a position to even get Manuel's attention.

I clung to the wheelhouse doorway and told myself there was no reason to be frightened. I was in a boat decorated with garlands of flowers, with lights, with streamers. I was in the company of an elderly couple, going to pick up another elderly woman. It was an unimaginably bright almost-summer day and I was in a harbor that was filled with boats and those boats were filled with happy people. Who's scared in the middle of the Portuguese Festival?

I, said the fly.

The marina at Fisherman's Wharf was renovated just a few years ago and has been doing a booming business ever since. There are something like a hundred slips there in the summertime, thanks to the floating docks, and some pretty impressive yachts get tied up there. Well, actually, some over-the-top-what-were-you-thinking yachts get tied up there. They weren't there now; they were all out in the harbor, settling into the boat parade conformation, and it was easy enough for the *Miss Maria* to sidle up to one of the docks. No rope ladder for Mrs. Mattos, of course; Manuel lowered a gangway while a couple of guys grabbed the lines and steadied the plank.

I looked around a little desperately. Now was my chance, if I really wanted to get off the boat. Now was Ali's chance to get *on* it, too, though there was no reason why he'd know we were there. The light and the tinted sky and water and boats and the noise were all melding into a kind of kaleidoscope of confused shapes and colors and I wondered, suddenly, if I were going to pass out. Not a very constructive response to the situation if I did.

And then Mrs. Mattos was hobbling down to us with a cane in one hand and leaning on some young guy I didn't know with the other. She looked grim and determined, though I'm not even sure what that looks like. Maybe it was an aura. I wasn't at all put off by it: I was desperately glad to just see someone I knew.

I wasn't thinking about Gerald. I couldn't think about Gerald. I would think about Gerald once I had the time and space for a nervous breakdown.

She glanced at me briefly as they hauled her onboard—there really wasn't another way to describe it—and then headed into the wheelhouse, where her greeting with her brother-in-law and his wife was about as effusive as a wildebeest catching sight of a lion. Or vice-versa.

Manuel meantime was bustling about on the deck, securing chairs and a couple of coolers and even a beach umbrella. He escorted Mrs. Mattos and then Sofia out and get them ensconced. Arsenio he ignored. Me, he leered at.

We were off to a smashing start.

Mrs. Mattos finally noticed me. "Where is he?" she demanded. "Your young man?"

"Your guess is as good as mine," I said flippantly. We were pulling away from the wharf and my stomach was turning over ominously. I've never been seasick in my life. I didn't think this had anything to do with seasickness.

She was staring at me and I shook off the flippancy. "Sorry, Mrs. Mattos. Just wondering what—"

She cut me off. "Is he coming?"

I swallowed hard against anything that might be considering coming up. "I don't know," I said helplessly. "I don't think so."

"He has to," she asserted.

Either her affection for my boyfriend was increasing exponentially or Ali was somehow part of her plan. Whatever her plan turned out to be. Either way, there was absolutely nothing I could do about it.

Hold on. I did still have a smartphone that was probably working even though my brain was apparently on the blink. I pulled it out and called Ali. "Where are you?"

"I was about to ask you the same question," I said. My relief at hearing his voice was nearly overwhelming. "Ali, I don't know if you heard, Gerald Wolff—"

He cut me off. "I know," he said. Terse. "We can talk about it later."

"But—"

"I'm just leaving Flyer's," he said. "I saw you out in the harbor, kid gave me his binoculars. Are you all right?"

"Yes, but what—"

"Do me a favor," he said. "Don't say anything else. I'll get out to you. Just sit there and don't do anything and don't say anything about Wolff."

If he'd given me those instructions under normal circumstances, I've had told him where to stow them. As it was, since my body couldn't decide if it wanted to cry or throw up or both, I just nodded numbly. "Okay."

"Okay. Sydney. Listen. I'll be there as soon as I can. Babe, listen. Listen to me. You're going to be all right." It was Ali's version of *breathe, Riley, just breathe.*

"Okay," I said.

"Okay. See you soon. Bye."

I clicked off and turned back to Mrs. Mattos. "He'll be here," I told her.

She nodded impassively, a small elderly Buddha. "Good."

There was music coming now from Mac-Millan Wharf as the Portuguese bands struck up. The procession would be coming, the priests, the Knights of Columbus, the whole community, the statue of Saint Peter, patron saint of fishermen, in pride of place at the head of it all. The boats were lining up, jockeying for position.

The Blessing of the Fleet. The center of the town's history.

I allowed myself to look around. The other fishing boats were all around us, dressed in their finery, their Sunday best. You didn't see the toil and terror that went into what they did, the waves crashing onto the deck, the hauls that filled their holds and the ones that didn't. The ten to twelve hours on deck in heavy-duty rain gear, the sleep caught in increments of one or two or maybe four hours, the constant awareness of plying one of the most dangerous trades on the planet. The dollar taped up in the cabin with the Sharpie inscription, "This is why we're here." The mistakes that you never come back from. The blood and the pain and the exhaustion.

Today, all you saw was the beauty. Scrubbed decks, freshened paint, polished metal. You looked at these boats and you could just about imagine what they saw out there, the beauty of it, the beauty of hard work and living off the sea, the beauty of long peaceful sunsets and the screaming of the herring gulls at dawn. Rounding Long Point Light and knowing you were nearly home.

I found myself unconsciously breathing more deeply, as though I could feel the winds of Stellwagen and the immensity of the ocean. It felt… good, in the midst of everything, it felt good. It was a reason to be here, on the water. It was a reason to live here, in Provincetown.

One of the Dolphin Fleet whaleboats came up beside us and slid past, the naturalist for once not talking about flukes and baleens but about the Portuguese heritage of the town. I steadied myself and kept breathing. This was sacred time, time apart, and the only way I was going to get through this day would be to become part of that. Not the other.

"Oh, shit," said Manuel. He was looking over his right shoulder, and when I turned, it was a Coast Guard boat I saw nosing its way through, no siren, but blue lights flashing.

Standing on the deck was Ali.

21

We all looked so friendly, I thought.

Manuel had ceded steering in the wheel-house to a captain from one of his other boats, a guy he called Jack, and had joined us on deck. There were cups filled with some kind of sweet wine. There was even laughter, as Sofia pointed out something on another boat and Arsenio roused himself enough to show his appreciation of it.

Ali had his arm around my shoulders. "Gerald," I'd said to him when he got on board, and he grabbed me and held me. "Later," he said softly. "We have to talk about it later."

The bishop was standing on his balcony on the *Provincetown II*. The music was playing. The boats were all sounding their horns, a cacophony of delight. The parade was moving along, the holy water hardly noticeable as it was cast but somehow *there*, important, significant. We passed under it slowly and, to my surprise, uneventfully.

Maybe I'd been wrong. Maybe all this had been my imagination. Maybe Mrs. Mattos had just wanted us here to celebrate, or to remember, or to… damned if I knew what else.

But then I glanced around the people on the *Miss Maria*'s deck and knew I'd been right.

Mrs. Mattos waited until we'd cleared the pier and then called Manuel over to her, his head close to hers so he could hear her. He didn't look happy; she looked determined. "Let's go inside," he said, finally, to everyone, and we all slowly, hesitantly followed him into the wheelhouse. It took a while; Ali and I had to help the older people. When I was in my eighties, I decided, I didn't want to be out on a boat for the Blessing.

The guy at the wheel was steering us away from the pier, away from the parade, away from the other boats. The noise gradually diminished. *Oh, God*, I thought, looking at Mrs. Mattos. *This is a Hercule Poirot moment after all.* And then: *this is a Very Bad Idea.*

Breathe, Riley, breathe.

Manuel was watching her, and he looked uncomfortable as hell; he had to know what was coming. Given the people assembled, unless Ali or I had become suspects in a murder that had happened before either of us was born, everyone had to know what was coming.

Mrs. Mattos didn't waste any time. "You killed Maria," she said. Exactly what I'd expected, by now, to hear.

Except that she was talking to Sofia.

***

Ali, perhaps predictably, reacted first. He moved away from me until he was standing—still casually, if that were possible—between the two women. Sofia was sitting in one of the chairs next to her husband; Mrs. Mattos was on the hard bench that ran down one side of the wheelhouse. Ali made his move look natural.

I cleared my throat. "How do you know?"

Manuel said, "That's impossible."

Mrs. Mattos didn't even glance at either of us. "You killed her an' then you an' Arsenio and my Duarte put her in my house. In *my house*. Probably you've all been laughing

269

about that for years, haven't you? Thinking, oh, that Emilia, don't even know that Maria's been with her all this time!" She paused. "What I can't figure out is why she went to you. She shoulda come to me. She shoulda come to me, and she'd still be alive now."

Sofia said, "She loved me more. That's why she came to me."

"Wait," Ali said. He turned to Sofia. "You understand what Emilia's saying?" he asked. "You don't have to say anything—"

"Don't matter," said Sofia. Her chin was jutting out aggressively.

Manuel was staring at Sofia. "This isn't true," he said, his voice flat. "You said she wrote to you. You said she run off with that—"

"Of course I said that," she snapped. "What was I gonna say? Of course I said she'd gone to New York. And you can stop lookin' at me like that, Manuel Silva, 'cause you of all people should be grateful for what I done!"

He shouted at her. "*Grateful?*" Everyone jumped slightly. "Grateful? I loved her!"

Join the club, I thought. Half the problems of this town, it seemed, had come from too many people loving Maria Mattos.

"She was gonna have some other man's baby!" Sofia spat the words out. "He wasn't one of us!"

"Jack," Ali said, "turn the boat around. We're going back in."

"No," said Arsenio, "we're not." I had just about decided that he was mute. Now everyone looked at him and there was a very large pistol in his hand. Oh, *hell*.

Sofia said, with satisfaction, "Arsenio was in Vietnam. He knows how to use that." Don't make any mistake, her tone said. An old man with a gun is still a man with a gun.

Mrs. Mattos didn't seem disturbed by any of it. "How did you do it?" she asked. "Only part of it I can't figure out."

"Pillow over her face," Sofia said with satisfaction. "She was asleep. She came when that fellow left, an' she said she'd go ahead, marry Manny, get on with things. I was happy about it, too, I can tell you. Then she told me about the baby."

"I already knew," said Mrs. Mattos with satisfaction. "She told me weeks before that." If it weren't absurd, it would have sounded like middle-school one-upmanship.

"More fool you, then," said Sofia. "She was the closest I had to a daughter. She *was* my daughter. So she was my responsibility. I wasn't gonna let that happen."

"Let what happen?" asked Manuel, his voice anguished. "It would have been all right in the end. It would have."

"Not in my family," she said grimly. "I gave her some supper and a pill to help her sleep. She was happy enough to be there. She said she was gonna go and see Manny the next day, put everything right."

Maria had had no way of knowing that Gerald planned to come back for her. And even if she did... I could see her standing on MacMillan, looking out into the harbor, realizing it had been a fling, her and the trust-fund baby. I could see her deciding that Provincetown was home, and a fishing family her future.

It wasn't a bad decision.

Manuel looked like he was ready to kill Sofia with his bare hands. He probably could, too. "How did you do it?" I asked, to distract him. Okay, maybe asking someone how they killed the fiancée of a strong angry man isn't the world's best distraction, but it was the best I could do in the circumstances. "I mean, didn't she struggle?" Even drugged, Maria had been sixteen and probably strong. Of course, Sofia in her thirties had probably been able to handle just about anything.

She shrugged. "Arsenio was there, just in case."

Manuel looked across at the older man. "But not to do it?"

Sofia answered him. "She was my responsibility," she said again.

Arsenio, I concluded, might have been a fine fisherman and provider, but on the home front he definitely lived in Sofia's shadow. And she'd cast a long one, up through half a century. I wondered if she was relieved to finally be talking about it. Certainly she didn't seem to be experiencing any regrets.

I could imagine the dark, the hurried conversation, Arsenio heading through the sleeping night streets to wake his brother. Bringing Duarte back to the house on Court Street, Sofia's adrenaline still pumping, the men's consternation. Her resolve. She was the one, I thought, who had the idea of walling Maria up. The men had fishing boats, for cripes' sake. They could have taken her down to the harbor, gotten her on board, dropped her body out at sea. They knew the currents; they knew how to make sure she didn't wash up before the fish had had their way with her.

No; that was Sofia. She must have really, *really* hated Emilia Mattos. I didn't know Duarte but if he were anything like his brother he'd have let her do all the planning. Surprise Emilia with a bathroom. The cousins would love to see her and Tony, why not send them there? What, Tony wants to go to camp? Perfect. No, you're not going fishing for a couple of weeks, you're both staying home and getting this done.

Ali was paying attention to Arsenio. "The gun," he said calmly. "Probably not a good idea."

Arsenio jerked his head toward his wife. "Gotta take care of her," he said.

"Not the best way," said Ali, his voice still even, still pleasant. He moved again, crossing the wheelhouse so that he was standing in the doorway, close to Manuel. He knew, already, who was most likely to lose it.

Sofia said, "We're all better off without her."

Manuel made a sound that was barely human, a roar of pain and anger and God only knew what, and he moved across the wheelhouse blindingly fast, heading for Sofia.

The gun went off, deafening in the small space, and Ali cursed and suddenly he wasn't in the doorway anymore, he was toppling outside onto the deck and over the edge of the side.

I didn't think. For the second time in two days, I went after him.

Straight overboard and into the harbor.

The water closed over my head. And, God, was it cold. I came up to the surface gasping and panicking. "Ali!" He wasn't dead. He couldn't be dead. He was here some-where, I just had to find him. "Ali!" I screamed again.

And then I had it: he was a few feet away, the dark hair bobbing just over the swell. It took forever to get to him, every wave push-ing me farther away it seemed. "Ali!" I gasped, hooking my arm around him, keeping his head above water. I had no idea whether or not he was alive. He had to be. He *had* to be.

The air around me filled, suddenly, with a roar, the sound of nightmares, and the water felt alive with currents. For a moment I thought a whale was surfacing and we were going to be drowned when it dived... And then my brain kicked in and recited the facts: the Boston boats don't stop for the Blessing. The huge catamaran fast-ferries that couldn't stop for anything were still plying the harbor.

We were directly in the channel.

And then there was another siren filling the air and one of the harbormaster boats was pulling up next to us and strong arms were pulling us up. "Let go of him, Sydney," John was saying. "It's okay, we've got it. We've got him. You gotta let go."

I flopped over onto my back, gasping. And then, unbelievably, I heard another voice. "Sunshine," Mirela said, "you just cannot keep yourself from jumping into the harbor, can you?"

22

Someone put one of those tinfoil-type blankets around my shoulders. They already had one on Ali, who was lying in the bottom of the boat; he wasn't conscious, but John from the harbormaster's was pressing down on his shoulder. He caught my eye. "He'll be okay," he said. John had been in Vietnam, too.

Mirela was sitting on the deck next to me. "You are all right?"

I nodded. "The *Miss Maria*—"

"She is already in, ahead of us," said Mirela.

I pulled the blanket closer around me. It might have been space-age material, but give me fleece any day. "And you're here... why, exactly?"

"Zack," she said. I blinked. "Your land-lord?" she reminded me.

"I know he's my landlord," I said. "I'm waiting to hear what my landlord has to do with this."

"Mrs. Mattos left a letter with him," she said. "In case—well, in case. She said to open it if she did not return, or if you did not."

"Cheerful thinking," I said. "And Zack be-ing Zack, he was a bit premature."

"He could not wait," she agreed. "But he did not want to call the police. At the end of the day, he thought I was best to go and see what had happened."

I managed a smile. "Thanks, Mirela." I looked across the boat. "I want to be next to Ali." I threw the blanket off. Mirela put her hand on my arm. "Wait," she said.

Something in her voice was off. "What?"

Mirela tightened her arm around me. "The *Miss Maria*," she said. "They boarded the *Miss Maria*."

"And?" And I knew that I knew.

"Mrs. Mattos," she said.

"Arsenio shot her?"

She shook her head and grimaced as we hit a particularly hard bump in the waves. "It was a heart attack, sunshine," she said. "It was probably quick."

No, I thought. No more Mrs. Mattos. No more kale soup or trips to Stop & Shop or gossip in the middle of Carver Street. Another part of this town's history gone.

She'd gotten to the pier before we did, and there was already canvas covering her body. An ambulance was there, too, ready for Ali, to take him to the hospital in Hyannis.

"Miss? We have to check you out."

Mirela was next to me. "I will stay with Mrs. Mattos," she said. "You go."

I climbed into the ambulance beside Ali and realized he was awake and looking at me.

"Thanks."

I managed a small smile. We were lucky. Too many people had died behind this one death. Maria, Hubert, Gerald, Emilia Mattos... I shivered. The next time I went into that harbor, I decided, it would be for the Swim for Life, and I'd be wearing a wetsuit.

"Don't do it again," said Ali.

The End

Author's Note

The names Costa, Silva, Cabral, Santos, etc. resonate throughout the history of Provincetown. Members of these families built the town, protected it from fire and flood, sailed its vessels, taught its children, and nursed its elderly. Without including these names, I could not offer an authentic atmosphere that truly reflected the vitality, humor, and grace that is Provincetown's Portuguese community. And without speaking to the history that they forged here I cannot adequately paint a picture of what it means to live in a fishing village.

That said, this book is a work of fiction. All similarities to any individual are coincidental—with the exception of people in public positions or who have kindly allowed me to use their names—and the events within are not intended reflect the real-life experiences of any of my friends and neighbors.

Acknowledgments

So many people contributed to this, as they do to every book in this series: the people of Provincetown (and elsewhere!) are amazingly generous.

In no particular order, I owe a debt of gratitude to Margo Nash, Dianne Kopser, Garr Roosma, Colin Kegler, Napi Van Derek, Jennifer Cabral, Rex McKinsey, Lady Di, Charlotte Rogers, Claire Gold, Nan Cinnater, Deb Karacozian, Miladinka Milic, Pat Medina, Mike Miller, Matt Clark, Peter, Rob, and Sofia.

As always. Homeport Press is the best publisher ever. Thanks for everything, Buck.

Did You Enjoy This Book?

If you did...

1) please share your opinion on Goodreads, Amazon, BN.com, and Powell's.

2) visit my Amazon page and read some of my other books.

3) give the book a boost on by telling people about it on Facebook and Twitter.

4) subscribe to The Novelist's Notebook at www.JeannettedeBeauvoir.com (scroll to bottom of page) for book reviews, short stories, quizzes, free stuff, previews of upcoming work, and more.

5) ask your local bookseller to stock *The Deadliest Blessing*

6) make it your choice for your next book-club meeting (I'll even join you by Skype or Zoom if you'd like me to!)

7) email me at JeannettedeBeauvoir@gmail.com and tell me so!

8) And watch for the next in the P'town Theme Week series from Homeport Press!